From the astonishing casebook of "the world's best-selling author":

A blood-red kiss for a dead man's betrayal.

Chinese vengeance from the fingers of Fong.

The man in a dog collar who got back his courage.

A fearful train ride to outwit a thief.

A blackmail-murder that took care of a tart—and put several people outside the law.

THE CASE OF THE CRIMSON KISS
was originally published by
William Morrow & Company, Inc.

ERLE STANLEY

GARDNER

THE CASE OF THE CRIMSON KISS

A PERRY MASON NOVELETTE
AND OTHER STORIES

PUBLISHED BY POCKET BOOKS NEW YORK

THE CASE OF THE CRIMSON KISS

A Perry Mason Novelette and Other Stories

William Morrow edition published April, 1971
POCKET BOOK edition published April, 1972

This POCKET BOOK edition includes every word contained in the original, higher-priced edition. It is printed from brand-new plates made from completely reset, clear, easy-to-read type. POCKET BOOK editions are published by POCKET BOOKS, a division of Simon & Schuster, Inc., 630 Fifth Avenue, New York, N.Y. 10020.
Trademarks registered in the United States and other countries.

L

Standard Book Number: 671-77881-1.
Library of Congress Catalog Card Number: 70-142395.

This POCKET BOOK is published by arrangement with William Morrow & Company, Inc.

Printed in the U.S.A.

Contents

Publisher's Note

THE stories in this volume were selected from the vast store of Erle Stanley Gardner's work which has not appeared in book form before.

For those of his fans who knew him only as the creator of Perry Mason, Bertha Cool and Donald Lam (mysteries written under the pseudonym of A. A. Fair), or Doug Selby, the D.A., it may come as a surprise to discover the variety of characters and situations appearing in stories he wrote for the magazines.

For our selection here, in addition to one novelette featuring Perry Mason, we chose four stories, written early in the author's career, which clearly indicate his extraordinary inventiveness and range of interests.

As a struggling young lawyer in Oxnard, California, Gardner became known as the defender of the Chinese, a minority group then considered beneath the dignity of rights unalienable to others. Thus began an interest in the Oriental that lasted throughout his life and which found expression in a number of short stories, among them *Fingers of Fong*.

From his earliest days, Gardner was lured by the desert and spent as much time there as he could snatch from the rigorous schedule imposed by his success as "the world's best-selling author." His love and respect for these arid reaches of the West emerge through the pages of *The Valley of Little Fears*.

Crooked Lightning unfolds as deviously and sharply as its title and forks at the end with that special twist characteristic of Gardner's work.

Although Jerry Marr, the protagonist in *At Arm's Length,* is a private detective, there is a tough-mindedness in his approach and brilliance in his deduction that suggest a step in the evolution of Perry Mason.

And last, but in sequential order, first, *The Case of the Crimson Kiss,* a novelette which saw light of day in the June 1948 issue of *American* magazine, brings us full circle to Perry Mason—quintessence of Erle Stanley Gardner's unique career.

The Case of the Crimson Kiss

CHAPTER ONE

PREOCCUPATION with her own happiness prevented Fay Allison from seeing the surge of bitter hatred in Anita's eyes.

So Fay, wrapped in the warmth of romantic thoughts, went babbling on to her roommate, her tongue loosened by the double cocktail which Anita had prepared before dinner.

"I'd known I loved him for a long time," she said, "but honestly, Anita, it never occurred to me that Dane was the marrying kind. He'd had that one unfortunate affair, and he'd always seemed so detached and objective about things. Of course, underneath all that reserve he's romantic and tender. Anita, I'm getting a break I don't deserve."

Anita Bonsal, having pushed her dinner plate to one side, toyed with the stem of her empty cocktail glass. Her eyes were pinpricks of black hatred which she was afraid to let Fay Allison see. "You've fixed a date?" she asked, concentrating on the rotating base of the glass.

"Just as soon as Aunt Louise can get here. I want her to be with me. I . . . and, of course, I'll want *you,* dear."

"When will Aunt Louise get here?"

"Tomorrow or the next day, I think. I haven't heard from her definitely."

"You've written her?"

"Yes. She'll take the night plane. I mailed her my extra key so she can come right on in whenever she gets here, even if we aren't here."

Anita Bonsal was silent, but Fay Allison wanted to talk. "You know how Dane is. He's always been sort of impersonal. He took *you* out at first as much as he did *me,* and then he began to specialize on me. Of course, you're so popular, you don't mind. It's different with me. Anita, I was afraid to acknowledge even to myself how deeply I felt, because I thought it might lead to heartache."

"All of my congratulations, dear," Anita said.

"Don't you think it will work out, Anita? You don't seem terribly enthusiastic."

"Of course it will work out. I'm not gushing because I'm a selfish devil and it's going to make a lot of difference in my personal life—the apartment and all that. Come on, let's get the dishes done. I'm going out tonight and I presume you'll be having company."

"No, Dane's not coming over. He's going through a ceremony at his bachelors' club—one of those silly things that men belong to. He has to pay a forfeit or something, and there's a lot of horseplay. I'm so excited, I'm just walking on air."

"Well," Anita said, "I go away for a three-day weekend and a lot seems to happen around here. I'll have to start looking for another roommate. This apartment is too big for me to carry by myself."

"You won't have any trouble. Just pick the person you want. How about one of the girls at the office?"

Anita shook her head, tight-lipped.

"Well, of course, I'll pay until the fifteenth and then . . ."

"Don't worry about that," Anita said lightly. "I'm something of a lone wolf at heart. I don't get along too well with most women, but I'll find someone. It'll take a little time for me to look around. Most of the girls in the office are pretty sappy."

They did the dishes and straightened up the apartment, Fay Allison talking excitedly, laughing with lighthearted merriment, Anita Bonsal moving with the swift efficiency of one who is deft with her hands, saying little.

As soon as the dishes had been finished and put away, Anita slipped into a black evening dress, put on her fur coat, smiled at Fay Allison, and said, "You'd better take some of the sleeping pills tonight, dear. You're all wound up."

Fay said somewhat guiltily, "I'm afraid I talked you to death, Anita. I wanted someone to listen while I built air castles. I . . . I'll read a book. I'll be waiting up when you get back."

"Don't," Anita said. "It'll be late."

Fay said wistfully, "You're always so mysterious about things, Anita. I really know very little about your friends. Don't you *ever* want to get married and have a home of your own?"

"Not me. I'm too fond of having my own way, and I like life as it is," Anita said, and slipped out through the door, gently pulling it shut behind her.

She walked down the corridor to the elevator, pressed the button, and when the cage came up to the sixth floor, stepped in and pressed the button for the lobby. She waited until the elevator was halfway down, pressed the stop button, then the button for the seventh floor.

The elevator rattled slowly upward and came to a stop.

Anita calmly opened her purse, took out a key, walked down the long corridor, glanced swiftly back toward the elevator, then fitted the key to apartment 702 and opened the door.

Carver L. Clements looked up from his newspaper, removed the cigar from his mouth, regarded Anita Bonsal with eyes that showed swift approval, but kept his voice detached as he said, "It took you long enough to get here."

"I had to throw a little wool in the eyes of my roommate and listen to her prattle of happiness. She's marrying Dane Grover."

Carver Clements put down the newspaper. "The hell she is!"

"It seems he went overboard in a burst of romance, and his attentions became serious and honorable," Anita said bitterly. "Fay has written her aunt, Louise Marlow, and as soon as the aunt gets here they'll be married."

Carver Clements shifted his position slightly, as though by doing so he could look at the tall brunette from a slightly different angle. "I had it figured out that you were in love with Dane Grover yourself."

"So that's been the trouble with you lately!"

"Weren't you?"

"Heavens, no!"

"You know, my love," Clements went on, "I'd hate to lose you now."

Anger blazed in her eyes. "Don't think you can own me!" she said sharply. "You only rent me."

"Let's call it a lease," he said.

"It's a tenancy-at-will," she flared. "And kindly get up when I come into the room. After all, you might as well show some manners."

Clements arose from the chair. He was a spidery man with long arms and legs, a thick, short body, a head almost bald, but he spent a small fortune on clothes that were skillfully cut to conceal the chunkiness of his body. He smiled and said, "My little spitfire! But I like you for it. Remember, Anita, I'm playing for keeps. As soon as I can get my divorce straightened out—"

"You and your divorce!" she interrupted. "You've been pulling that line . . ."

"It isn't a line. There are some very intricate property problems. I don't dare to seem too eager, and the thing can't be handled abruptly. You know that. You *should* know that."

"I know that I'm tired of all this pretense. I'm tired of

working. If you're playing for keeps, take me off the dole and make *me* a property settlement."

"And have my wife's lawyers suddenly drag me into court for another examination of my assets and start tracing the checks . . ."

"Make it in cash."

"And have the bank withdrawals checked? Don't be silly."

"I'm not going to be. I'm going to be practical. What if I should get dragged into your domestic mess anyway? Look at the chances *I'm* taking."

His eyes were somber in their steady appraisal. "I like you, Anita. I can do a lot for you. I like that fire that you have. But I want it in your heart and not in your tongue. My car's in the parking lot. You go on down, get in the car, and wait. I'll be down in five minutes."

She said, "Why don't you take me out as though you weren't ashamed of me? As though . . ."

"And give my wife the opportunity she's looking for? Then you *would* have the fat in the fire. The property settlement will be completed and signed within five or six weeks. Thank heavens, I'll then be free to live my own life in my own way. Until then . . . until then, my darling, we have to be discreet in our indiscretions."

She started to say something, checked herself, turned and stalked out of the apartment.

Carver Clements' automobile was a big luxurious sedan equipped with every possible convenience, but it was cold sitting there, waiting.

Anita waited for several minutes, then, as she felt the chill creeping through her sheer nylons, turned the ignition switch and pulled out the heater button.

It took a minute or two for warmth to generate in the heater. Then a welcome current of warm air swirled caressingly about her legs.

After ten minutes, which seemed twenty, she grew impatient. She flung open the car door, went to the entrance of the apartment house, and angrily pressed the button of 702.

When there was no answer, she assumed that Clements must be on his way down in the elevator, so she walked back into the shadows, to stand there, impatient, feeling a strange desire to smash something. But Clements didn't appear.

Anita used her key to enter the apartment house. The elevator was on the ground floor. She made no attempt at concealment this time, but pressed the button for the seventh floor, left the elevator, strode down the corridor, stabbed her key into the metal lock of Clements' apartment, and entered the room.

Carver L. Clements, dressed for the street, was lying sprawled on the floor.

A highball glass lay on its side two feet from his body. It had apparently fallen from his hand, spilling the contents as it rolled along the carpet. Clements' face was a peculiar hue, and there was a sharp, bitter odor which seemed intensified as she bent toward his froth-flecked lips. Since Anita had last seen him he had quite evidently had a caller. The print of half-parted lips flared in gaudy crimson from the front of his bald head.

With the expertness she had learned from a course in first aid, Anita pressed her finger against the wrist, searching for a pulse. There was none.

She opened her handbag, took out the silver cigarette case and held its smoothly polished surface close to the man's lips. There was no faintest sign of moisture which would indicate breathing.

Carver L. Clements, wealthy playboy, yachtsman, broker, gambler for high stakes, was quite dead.

In a panic Anita Bonsal looked through the apartment.

There were all too many signs of her surreptitious and intermittent occupancy of that apartment—nightgowns, lingerie, shoes, stockings, hats, even toothbrushes and her favorite toothpaste.

Anita Bonsal turned back toward the door and quietly

left the apartment. She paused in the hallway, making certain there was no one in the corridor. This time she didn't take the elevator, but walked down the fire stairs, as she had done so many times, and returned to her own apartment on the sixth floor.

Fay Allison had been listening to a musical program on the radio. She jumped up with glad surprise as Anita entered.

"Oh, Anita, I'm so glad! I thought—thought you wouldn't be in until real late. What happened? It hasn't been any time since you left."

"I developed a beastly headache," Anita said. "My escort was a trifle intoxicated, so I slapped his face and came home. I'd like to sit up and have you tell me about your plans, but I do have a headache, and you must get a good night's sleep tonight. You'll need to be looking your best tomorrow."

Fay laughed. "I don't want to waste time sleeping. While I'm unconscious I can't revel in my happiness."

"Nevertheless," Anita said firmly, "we're going to get to bed early. Let's undress, put on pajamas, have some hot chocolate, and then we'll sit in front of the electric heater and talk for just exactly twenty minutes."

"Oh, I'm so glad you came back!" Fay said.

"I'll fix the drink," Anita told her. "I'm going to make your chocolate sweet tonight. You can start worrying about your figure tomorrow. After all, you'll be a married woman before this chocolate can put any pounds on you."

She went to the kitchen, opened her purse, took out a bottle of barbiturate tablets, and emptied a good half of the pills into a cup. After she had carefully ground them she added hot water until they were, for the most part, dissolved.

She placed chocolate on the stove, added milk and melted marshmallows, and called out to Fay, "You undress, dear. I'll put on my pajamas after we've had the chocolate."

When she returned to the living room, carrying the two

steaming cups, frothy with melted marshmallows floating on top, Fay Allison was in her pajamas.

Anita Bonsal raised her cup. "Here's to happiness, darling."

"Lots of happiness," Fay Allison said almost dreamily.

After they had finished the first cup of chocolate, Anita talked Fay into another cup, then let Fay discuss her plans until drowsiness made the words thick, the sentences detached

Anita, I'm *so* sleepy all of a sudden. I guess it's the reaction from having been so keyed up. I . . . darling, it's all right if I . . . you don't care if I . . ."

"Not at all, dear," Anita said, and helped Fay into bed, tucked her in carefully, and then gave the situation careful consideration.

The fact that Carver Clements maintained a secret apartment in that building was known only to a few of his cronies. These people knew of Clements' domestic difficulties and knew why he maintained this apartment. Fortunately, however, they had never seen Anita. That was a big thing in her favor. Anita was quite certain it hadn't been a heart attack. It had been poison, some quick-acting, deadly poison. There was no use worrying herself, trying to figure out how it had been administered, or why. Carver Clements was a man who had many powerful friends and many powerful enemies.

The police would search for the woman.

It wouldn't do for Anita merely to remove her things from that apartment, and, besides, that wouldn't be artistic enough. Anita had been in love with Dane Grover. If it hadn't been for that dismal entanglement with Carver Clements . . . However, that was all past now, and Fay Allison, with her big blue eyes, her sweet, trusting disposition, had turned Dane Grover from a disillusioned wolf into an ardent suitor. Well, it was a world where the smart ones got by. Anita had washed the dishes. Fay Allison had dried them. Her fingerprints would be on glasses and on dishes. The management of the apartment house very considerately furnished dishes identical in pattern —and it only needed a little careful work on her part. She would, of course, put on gloves. The police would find Fay Allison's nightgowns in Carver Clements' secret apartment. They would find glasses that had Fay's fingerprints on them. And when they went to question Fay Allison, they would find she had taken the easy way out, an overdose of sleeping pills.

Anita would furnish the testimony that would make it all check into a composite, sordid pattern. A girl who had been the mistress of a rich playboy, then had met a younger and more attractive man who had offered her marriage. She had gone to Carver Clements and wanted to check out, but with Carver Clements one didn't simply check out. Things weren't as easy as that. So Fay had slipped the fatal poison into his drink and then had realized she was trapped when Anita returned home unexpectedly and there had been no chance for Fay to make surreptitious removal of her wearing apparel from the upstairs apartment. Anita would let the police do the figuring. Anita would be horrified, simply stunned, but, of course, cooperative.

Anita Bonsal deliberately waited three hours until things began to quiet down in the apartment house, then she took a suitcase and quietly went to work, moving with the smooth efficiency of a woman who has been accustomed to thinking out every smallest detail.

When she had finished, she carefully polished the key to apartment 702 so as to remove any possible fingerprints, and dropped it in Fay Allison's purse. She ground up all but six of the remaining sleeping tablets and mixed the powder with the chocolate which was left in the canister.

Then she donned pajamas, took the remaining six tablets, washed off the label with hot water, and tossed the empty bottle out of the back window of the apartment. Then she snuggled down into her own bed and switched off the lights.

Over in the other twin bed, Fay Allison lay motionless, except for a slight chest motion as her shallow breathing raised and lowered the coverlet.

The maid was due to come at eight the next morning to clean up the apartment. She would find two still figures, one dead, one in a drugged stupor.

Two of the tablets constituted the heaviest prescribed dose. The six tablets Anita had taken began to suck at her consciousness. For a moment there was swift panic. Perhaps she had really taken too many. Could it be that . . . that . . . perhaps . . .

It was too late now. The soothing influence of the drug warmed her consciousness into acquiescence.

She wondered if she could call a drugstore and find out if . . . a moment later she was asleep.

CHAPTER TWO

LOUISE MARLOW, tired from the long airplane ride, her ears still ringing with the sound of muffled motors, paid off the taxicab in front of the apartment house.

The cab driver surveyed her solicitously. "Want me to wait until you see if your party's home?"

"I have a key," Louise Marlow said.

"How about your bags?"

"Don't worry about them. I'll get them up all right."

He helped her with her bags to the entrance door. Louise Marlow inserted the key which Fay Allison had sent her, smiled her thanks to the cab driver, and picked up her bags.

Sixty-five years old, white-headed steely-eyed, square of shoulder and broad of beam, she had experienced many and varied vicissitudes in life, and from them had extracted a salty philosophy of her own. Her love was big enough to encompass those who were dear to her with a protecting umbrella. Her hatred was bitter enough to goad her enemies into confused retreat.

With casual disregard for the fact that it was now one o'clock in the morning, she marched calmly down the corridor to the elevator, banged her suitcase and overnight bag into the corner of the cage, and punched the button for the sixth floor.

The elevator moved slowly upward, then shuddered to a stop. The door slid slowly open and Aunt Louise, picking up her bags, walked down the half-darkened corridor, peering over the tops of her glasses for numbers over the doors.

At length she found the apartment she wanted, inserted her key, opened the door, and groped for a light switch.

She found the light switch, clicked it on, and called, "It's me, Fay!"

There was no answer.

Aunt Louise dragged her bags in, pushed the door shut, called out cheerfully, "Don't shoot," and then added by way of explanation, "I picked up a cancellation on an earlier plane, Fay."

The continued silence bothered her. She moved over to the bedroom.

"Wake up, Fay. It's your Aunt Louise!"

She clicked on the bedroom light, smiled down at the two sleepers, then said, "Well, if you're going to sleep right through everything, I'll make up a bed on the davenport and say hello to you in the morning."

Then something in the color of Fay Allison's face caused the keen eyes to lose their twinkle of friendly humor and become hard with steely concentration.

"Fay!" she said.

The figures slumbered on in complete oblivion.

Aunt Louise went over and shook Fay Allison, then turned to Anita Bonsal and started shaking her.

The motion finally brought Anita back to semiconsciousness from drugged slumber.

"Who is it?" she asked thickly.

"I'm Fay Allison's Aunt Louise. I got here ahead of time. What's happened?"

Anita Bonsal knew in a drowsy manner that this was a complicating circumstance that she had not foreseen, and despite the numbing effect of the drug on her senses, managed to mouth the excuse which was to be her first waking alibi.

"Something happened," she said thickly. "The chocolate . . . we drank chocolate and it felt like . . . I can't remember . . . can't remember . . . I want to go to sleep."

She let her head swing over on a limp neck and became a dead weight in Louise Marlow's arms.

Aunt Louise put her back on the bed, snatched up a telephone directory, and thumbed through the pages until she found the name—*Perry Mason, Attorney at Law.*

There was a night number—Westfield 6-5943.

Louise Marlow dialed the number.

The night operator on duty at the switchboard of the Drake Detective Agency, recognizing from the peculiar sound of the buzzing that the ringing phone was that of Mason's night number, picked up the receiver and said, "Night number of Mr. Perry Mason. Who is this talking, please?"

Louise Marlow said in a firm, steady voice, "This is Louise Marlow. I haven't met Perry Mason, but I know his secretary, Della Street. I want you to get in touch with her and tell her that I'm at Keystone nine-seven-six-oh-oh. I'm in a mess and I want her to call me back here just as quick as she can. Yes, that's right! I know her personally. You tell her it's Louise Marlow talking and she'll get busy. I think I may need Mr. Mason before I get through, but I certainly want to talk with Della Street right now."

Louise Marlow hung up and waited.

Within less than a minute she heard the phone ring, and Della Street's voice came over the line as Aunt Louise picked up the receiver and said, "Hello."

"Why, Louise Marlow, whatever are *you* doing in town?"

"I came in to attend the wedding of my niece, Fay

Allison," Aunt Louise said. "Now listen, Della. I'm at Fay's apartment. She's been drugged and I can't wake her up. Her roommate, Anita Bonsal, has also been drugged and I managed to get her awake, but she keeps going back to sleep. Someone's tried to poison them!

"I want to get a doctor who's good and who can keep his damned trap shut. I don't know what's back of all this, but Fay's getting married tomorrow. Someone's tried to put her under sod, and I propose to find out what's behind it. If anything should get into the newspapers about this, I'll wring someone's neck. The whole business looks fishy to me. I'm at the Mandrake Arms, apartment six-oh-four. Rush a doctor up here and then you'd better get hold of Perry Mason and . . ."

Della Street said, "I'll send a good doctor up to you right away, Mrs. Marlow. I just got in. Perry Mason, Paul Drake, the detective who handles his investigations, and I have been out nightclubbing with a client. Mr. Mason brought me home just a few minutes ago and I can catch him at his apartment. You sit tight. I'm getting busy."

CHAPTER THREE

WHEN Aunt Louise answered the buzzer, Della Street said, "Mrs. Marlow, this is Perry Mason. This is 'Aunt Louise,' chief. She's an old friend from my home town."

Louise Marlow gave the famous lawyer her hand and a smile. She kissed Della and said, "You haven't changed a bit, Della. Come on in. There's a mess here. I can't afford to have a word get in the newspapers. We had to get this sawbones. Now, how do we keep him from blabbing?"

"What does the doctor say?" Mason asked.

"He's working like a house afire. Anita is conscious. Fay is going to pull through all right. Another hour and it would have been too late for her."

"What happened?" Mason asked.

"Someone dumped sleeping medicine in the powdered chocolate, or else in the sugar."

"Any suspicions?" Mason asked.

"Fay was marrying Dane Grover. I gather from her letters he's a wealthy but shy young man who had one bad experience with a jane years ago and had turned bitter and disillusioned, or thought he had. A cynic at twenty-six! Baloney!"

Mason smiled.

"I got here around one o'clock, I guess. Fay had sent me a key. The place was closed tight as a miser's purse. I used the key. As soon as I switched on the light and looked at Fay's face, I knew that something was wrong, the color of it and the way she was breathing. I tried to wake her up and couldn't. I finally shook some sense into Anita. She said the chocolate did it. Then I called Della. That's just about all I know about it."

"The cups they drank the chocolate from?" Mason asked. "Where are they?"

"On the kitchen sink—unwashed."

"We may need them for evidence," Mason said.

"Evidence, my eye!" Louise Marlow snorted. "I don't want the police in on this. You can imagine what'll happen if some sob sister spills a lot of printer's ink about a bride-to-be trying to kill herself on the eve of the wedding."

"Let's take a look around," Mason said.

The lawyer moved about the apartment, trying to reconstruct what had happened.

Louise Marlow followed, acting as guide, and Della Street from time to time gave the benefit of a feminine suggestion.

Mason nodded, paused as he came to street coats thrown over the back of a chair, then again as he looked at the two purses.

"Which one is Fay Allison's?" he asked.

"Heavens, I don't know. We'll have to find out," Aunt Louise said.

Mason said, "I'll let you two take the lead. Go through them carefully. See if you can find anything that would indicate whether anyone might have been in the apartment shortly before they started drinking the chocolate. Perhaps there's a letter that will give us a clue, or a card or a note."

The doctor, emerging from the bedroom, said, "I want to boil some water for another hypo."

"How are they coming?" Mason asked, as Mrs. Marlow went to the kitchen.

"The brunette is all right," the doctor said, "and I think the blonde will make it all right."

"When can I question one of them in detail?"

The doctor shook his head. "I wouldn't advise it. Not that it will hurt anything, but you might get thrown off the track. They are still groggy, and there's some evidence that the brunette is rambling and contradictory in her statements. Give her another hour and you can get some facts. Right now she's running around in circles."

The doctor boiled water for his hypo and went back to the bedroom. Della Street moved over to Mason's side and said in a low voice, "Here's something I don't understand, chief."

"What?"

"Notice the keys to the apartment house are stamped with the numbers of the apartments. Both girls have keys to this apartment in their purses. Fay Allison also has a key stamped seven-oh-two. What would she be doing with the key to another apartment?"

Mason's eyes narrowed for a moment in thoughtful speculation. "What does Aunt Louise say?"

"She doesn't know. I was the one who searched Fay's purse. She went through Anita's."

"Anything else to give a clue?"

"Not the slightest thing anywhere."

Mason said, "Okay, I'm going to take a look at seven-oh-two. You'd better come along, Della."

Mason made excuses to Louise Marlow. "We want to

look around awhile on the outside," he said. "We'll be back in a few minutes."

He and Della took the elevator to the seventh floor, walked down to apartment 702, and Mason pushed his thumb against the bell button.

They could hear the sound of the buzzer in the apartment, but there was no sound of answering motion such as would have been caused by sleepers stirring around.

Mason said, "It's a chance we shouldn't take, but I'm going to take a peek inside, just for luck."

He fitted the key to the door, clicked back the lock, and gently opened the door.

The blazing lights of the living room streamed illumination out at them through the open door, showed the sprawled body on the floor, the drinking glass which had rolled from the dead fingers.

The door from an apartment across the hall jerked open. A young woman with disheveled hair, a bathrobe around her, said angrily, "After you've pressed a buzzer that long at this time of the night you should have sense enough to—"

"We have," Mason interrupted, pulling Della Street into the apartment and kicking the door shut behind them with a quick jab of his heel.

Della Street, clinging to Mason's arm, saw the sprawled figure on the floor, the crimson lipstick on the forehead. She looked at the overturned chair by the table, the glass which had rolled along the carpet, spilling part of its contents, and at the other empty glass standing on the table across from the overturned chair.

Her breathing was heavy and fast, as though she had been running, but she said nothing.

"Careful, Della, we mustn't touch anything."

"Who is he?"

"Apparently he's People's Exhibit A. Do you suppose the nosy dame in the opposite apartment is out of the hall by this time? We'll have to take a chance anyway."

He wrapped his hand with his handkerchief, turned the knob on the inside of the door, and pulled it silently open.

The door of the apartment across the hall was closed.

Mason warned Della Street to silence with a gesture. They tiptoed out into the corridor, pulling the door closed behind them.

As the door clicked shut, the elevator came to a stop at the seventh floor. Three men and a woman came hurrying down the corridor directly toward them.

Mason's voice was low, reassuring. "Perfectly casual, Della. Just friends departing from a late card game."

They caught the curious glances of the four people, moved slightly to one side, then, after the quartet had passed, Mason took Della Street's arm and said, "Don't hurry, Della, take it easy."

"Well," Della Street said, "they'll certainly know us if they ever see us again. The way that woman looked me over . . ."

"I know," Mason said, "but we'll hope that . . . oh, oh!"

"What is it?"

"They're going to seven-oh-two!"

The four paused in front of the door. One of the men pressed the buzzer button.

Almost immediately the door of the opposite apartment jerked open. The woman with the bathrobe shrilled, "I'm suffering from insomnia. I've been trying to sleep, and this—"

She broke off as she saw the strangers.

The man who had been pressing the button grinned and said in a booming voice which carried well down the corridor, "We're sorry, ma'am. I only just gave him one short buzz."

"Well, the other people who went in just before you made enough commotion."

"Other people *in here?*" the man asked, hesitated a

moment, then went on. "Well, we won't bother him if he's got company."

Mason pulled Della Street into the elevator, pulled the door shut, and pushed the button for the lobby.

"What in the world do we do now?" Della Street asked.

"Now," Mason said, his voice sharp-edged with disappointment, "we ring police headquarters and report a possible homicide. It's the only thing we *can* do. The woman only saw two people she can't identify going *in,* but that quartet will eventually identify us as going out."

There was a phone booth in the lobby. Mason dropped in a coin, dialed police headquarters, and reported that he had found a corpse in apartment 702 under circumstances indicating probable homicide. He had, he said, touched nothing but had backed right out and called the police.

While Mason was in the phone booth, the four people emerged from the elevator. There was a distinct aroma of alcohol as they pushed their way toward the door. The woman, catching sight of Della Street standing beside the phone booth, favored her with a feminine appraisal which swept from head to foot and missed no smallest detail.

Mason called Louise Marlow in apartment 604. "I think you'd better have the doctor take his patients to a sanitarium where they can have complete quiet," he said.

"He seems to think they're doing all right here."

"I distrust doctors who *seem* to think," Mason said. "I would suggest a sanitarium immediately, and *complete quiet.*"

Louise Marlow was silent for a full three seconds.

"Are you there?" Mason asked.

"I'm here," she said. "I'm just trying to get the sketch."

"I think the patients should have *complete quiet,*" Mason said.

"Damn it," Louise Marlow sputtered. "When you said it the first time I missed it. The second time I got it. You don't have to let your needle get stuck on the record! I was just trying to figure it out."

Mason heard her slam up the phone at the other end of the line.

Mason grinned and hung up the phone. Then he took the key to 702 from his pocket, dropped it in an envelope, addressed the envelope to his office, stamped it, and dropped it in the mailbox by the elevator.

Outside, the four people in the car were having something of an argument. Apparently there was some sharp difference of opinion as to what action was to be taken next, but as a siren sounded they reached a sudden unanimity of decision. They were starting the car when the police car pulled in to the curb. The red beam of the police spotlight pilloried them. The siren blasted a peremptory summons.

The driver of the car looked behind him, then stepped on the gas.

The police car shot away in angry pursuit, and three minutes later a chastened quartet swung their car back to a stop in front of the apartment house, the police car following them until the machine was safely parked at the curb. One of the radio officers walked over to the other car, took possession of the ignition keys, and ushered the four people up to the door of the apartment house.

Mason hurried across the lobby to open the locked door.

The officer said, "I'm looking for a man who reported a body."

"That's right. I did. My name's Mason. The body's in seven-oh-two."

"A body!" the woman screamed.

"Shut up," the radio officer said.

"But *we* know the . . . why he told you we'd been visiting in seven-oh-two . . . we . . ."

"Yeah, you said you'd been visiting a friend in seven-oh-two, name of Carver Clements. How was he when you left him?"

There was an awkward silence, then the woman said, "We *really* didn't get in. We just went to the door. The woman across the way said he had company, so we left."

"Said he had company?"
"That's right. But *I* think the company had left. It was these two here."
"We'll go take a look," the officer said. "Come on."

CHAPTER FOUR

LIEUTENANT TRAGG, head of the Homicide Squad, finished his examination of the apartment and said wearily to Mason, "I presume by this time you've thought up a good story to explain how it all happened."
Mason said, "As a matter of fact, I don't know this man from Adam. I had never seen him alive."
"I know," Tragg said sarcastically, "you wanted him as a witness to an automobile accident or something, and just happened to drop around in the wee small hours of the morning."
Mason said nothing.
"But," Tragg went on, "strange as it may seem, Mason, I'm interested to know how you got in. The woman who has the apartment across the corridor says you stood there and rang the buzzer for as much as two minutes. Then she heard the sound of a clicking bolt just as she opened her door to give you a piece of her mind, thinking you were some drunken bum trying to buzz a girl friend who had cooled off on him."
Mason nodded gravely.
Tragg said, "Either someone opened that door or the door was open. If it was ajar, I don't think you'd have buzzed for two minutes without pushing it open. If someone was in there, I want to know who it was. Now who let you in?"
"I had a key."
"A key! The hell you did!"
Mason nodded.
"Let's take a look at it."
"I'm sorry, I don't have it now."

"Well, now," Tragg said, *"isn't* that interesting! And where did you get the key, Mason?"

"Unfortunately," Mason said, *"that's* something I can't tell you."

"Don't be silly. This is a murder case."

Mason said, "The key came into my possession in a peculiar manner. I found it."

"Phooey! A client gave it to you."

"What makes you think that?"

"It's a reasonable conjecture."

Mason smiled. "Come, come, Lieutenant, if you're going to engage in pure flights of fancy, why not consider the possibility that this client might have taken a sublease on the apartment and wanted me to see that the gentleman lying there on the floor, who was unlawfully withholding possession, was ejected without trouble?"

"So you came to eject him at this time in the morning!"

"Perhaps the sublease didn't become effective until midnight."

Tragg's eyes narrowed. "It's a nice try, Mason, but you're not getting anywhere. That key you have is the dead man's key. When we searched the body we found that stuff on the table there. There's no key to this apartment on him."

Mason sparred for time said, "And did you notice that despite the face there's a thermos jar of ice cubes on the table, a bottle of Scotch, and a siphon of soda, the fatal drink didn't have any ice in it?"

"How do you know?" Tragg asked, interested.

"Because when this glass fell from his hand and the contents spilled over the floor, it left a single small spot of moisture. If there had been ice cubes in the glass, they'd have rolled out for some appreciable distance and then melted, leaving spots of moisture."

"I see," Tragg said sarcastically. "And then, having decided to commit suicide, the guy kissed himself on the forehead and . . ."

He broke off as one of the detectives, walking rapidly down the hallway, said, "We've traced that cleaning mark, Lieutenant."

Tragg glanced significantly toward Mason and said, "I'll talk with you in a minute when . . ."

The man handed Tragg a folded slip of paper.

Tragg unfolded the paper. "Well I'll be damned!" he said.

Mason met Tragg's searching eyes with calm steadiness.

"And I suppose," Tragg said, "you're going to be surprised at this one. Miss Fay Allison, apartment six-oh-four, in this same building, is the person who sent the coat that was in the closet to the dry cleaner. Her mark is on it. I think, Mr. Mason, we'll have a little talk with Fay Allison, and just to see that you don't make any false moves until we get there, we'll take you right along with us. Perhaps you already know the way."

As Tragg started toward the elevator, a smartly dressed woman in her late thirties or early forties stepped out of the elevator and walked down the corridor, looking at the numbers over the doors.

Tragg stepped forward. "Looking for something?"

She started to sweep past him.

Tragg pulled back his coat, showing her his badge.

"I'm looking for apartment seven-oh-two," she said.

"Who are you looking for?"

"Mr. Carver Clements, if it's any of your business."

"I think it is," Tragg said. "Who are you and how do you happen to be here?"

"I am Mrs. Carver L. Clements, and I'm here because I was advised over the telephone that my husband was maintaining a surreptitious apartment here."

"And that was the first you knew of it?"

"Definitely."

"And what," Tragg asked, "did you intend to do?"

"I intend to show him that he isn't getting away with anything," she said. "If you're an officer, you may as well accompany me. I feel certain that . . ."

Tragg said, "Seven-oh-two is down the corridor, at the corner on the right. I just came from there. You'll find a detective there in charge of things. Your husband was killed sometime between seven and nine o'clock."

Dark-brown eyes grew wide with surprise. "You . . . you're sure?"

Tragg said, "Dead as a mackerel. Someone slipped him a little cyanide, in his Scotch and soda. I don't suppose you'd know anything about that?"

She said slowly, "If my husband is dead . . . I can't believe it. He hated me too much to die. He was trying to force me to make a property settlement, and in order to make me properly submissive, he'd put me through a softening-up process, a period during which I didn't have money enough even to dress decently. His idea was that that would make the settlement he was prepared to offer look practically irresistible to me."

"In other words," Tragg said, "you hated his guts."

She clamped her lips together. "I didn't say that!"

Tragg grinned and said, "Come along with us. We're going down to an apartment on the sixth floor. After that I'm going to take *your* fingerprints and see if they match up with those on the glass which didn't contain the poison."

CHAPTER FIVE

LOUISE MARLOW answered the buzzer.

She glanced at Tragg, then at Mrs. Clements.

Mason, raising his hat, said with grave politeness and the manner of a total stranger, "We're sorry to bother you at this hour, but . . ."

"I'll do the talking," Tragg said.

The formality of Mason's manner was not lost on Aunt Louise. She said, as though she had never seen him before, "Well, this is a great time . . ."

Tragg pushed his way forward. "Does Fay Allison live here?"

"That's right," Louise Marlow beamed at him. "She and another girl, Anita Bonsal, share the apartment. They aren't here now, though."

"Where are they?" Tragg asked.

She shook her head. "I'm sure I couldn't tell you."

"And who are you?"

"I'm Louise Marlow, Fay Allison's aunt."

"You're living with them?"

"Heavens, no. I just came up to be here for . . . for a visit with Fay."

"How did you get in, if they weren't here?"

"I had a key, but I didn't say they weren't here then."

"You said, I believe, that they are not here now?"

"That's right."

"What time did you arrive?"

"Around one o'clock this morning."

Tragg said, "Let's cut out the shadowboxing and get down to brass tacks, Mrs. Marlow. I want to see both of those girls."

"I'm sorry, but the girls are both sick. They're in the hospital."

"Who took them there?"

"A doctor."

"What's his name?"

Louise Marlow hesitated a moment, then said, "It's just a simple case of food poisoning. Only . . ."

"What's the doctor's name?"

"Now you listen to me," Louise Marlow said. "I tell you, these girls are too sick to be bothered, and—"

Lieutenant Tragg said, "Carver L. Clements, who has an apartment on the floor above here, is dead. It looks like murder. Fay Allison had evidently been living up there in the apartment with him and . . ."

"What are you talking about?" Louise Marlow exclaimed indignantly. "Why, I . . . I . . ."

"Take it easy," Tragg said. "Her clothes were up there. There's a laundry mark that has been traced to her."

"Clothes!" Louise Marlow snorted. "Why, it's probably some junk she gave away somewhere, or . . ."

"I'm coming to that," Lieutenant Tragg said patiently. "I don't want to do anyone an injustice. I want to play it on the up-and-up. Now then, there are fingerprints in that apartment, the fingerprints of a woman on a drinking glass, on the handle of a toothbrush, on a tube of toothpaste. I'm not going to get tough unless I have to, but I want to get hold of Fay Allison long enough to take a set of rolled fingerprints from her hands. You try holding out on me, and see what the newspapers have to say tomorrow."

Louise Marlow reached an instant decision. "You'll find her at the Crestview Sanitarium," she said, "and if you want to make a little money, I'll give you odds of a hundred to one, in any amount you want to take, that—"

"I'm not a betting man," Tragg said dryly. "I've been in this game too long."

He turned to one of the detectives and said, "Keep Perry Mason and his charming secretary under surveillance and away from a telephone until I get a chance at those fingerprints. Okay, boys, let's go."

CHAPTER SIX

PAUL DRAKE, head of the Drake Detective Agency, pulled a sheaf of notes from his pocket as he settled down in the client's chair in Mason's office.

It was ten-thirty in the morning, and the detective's face showed signs of weariness as he assumed his favorite crosswise position in the big leather chair, with his long legs hanging over one overstuffed arm, the small of his back propped against the other.

"It's a mess, Perry," he said.

"Let's have it," Mason said.

"Fay Allison and Dane Grover were going to get married today. Last night Fay and Anita Bonsal, who shares the apartment with her, settled down in front of the fireplace for a nice gabby little hen party. They made chocolate. Both girls had been watching their figures, but this was a celebration. Fay felt she could really let loose. She had two cups of chocolate, Anita had one. Fay evidently got about twice the dose of barbiturate that Anita did. Both girls passed out.

"Next thing Anita knew, Louise Marlow, Fay's aunt, was trying to wake her up. Fay Allison didn't recover consciousness until after she was in the sanitarium.

"The rest of the stuff you know pretty well.

"Anyhow, Tragg went out and took Fay Allison's fingerprints. They check absolutely with those on the glass. What the police call the murder glass is the one that slipped from Carver Clements' fingers and rolled around the floor. It had been carefully wiped clean of all fingerprints. Police can't even find one of Clements' prints on it. The other glass on the table had Fay's prints. It's her toothbrush. The closet was filled with her clothes. She was living there with him. It's a hell of a stink.

"Dane Grover is standing by her, but I personally don't think he can stand the gaff much longer. When a man's engaged to a girl and the newspapers scream the details of her affair with a wealthy playboy all over the front pages, you can't expect the man to appear exactly nonchalant. The aunt, Louise Marlow, tells me he's being faced with terrific pressure to repudiate the girl, publicly break the engagement, and take a trip.

"The girls insist it's all part of some sinister overall plan to frame them, that they were drugged, and all that, but how could anyone have planned it that way? For instance, how could anyone have known they were going to take the chocolate in time to—"

"The chocolate was drugged?" Mason asked.

Drake nodded. "They'd used up most of the chocolate,

but the small amount left in the package is pretty well doped with barbiturate."

Mason began toying with a lead pencil.

"The police theory," Drake went on, "is that Fay Allison had been playing house with Carver Clements. She wanted to get married. Clements wouldn't let her go. She slipped him a little poison. She intended to return and get her things out of the apartment when it got late enough so she wouldn't meet someone in the corridor if she came walking out of seven-oh-two with her arms full of clothes. Anita, who had gone out, unexpectedly returned, and that left Fay Allison trapped. She couldn't go up and get her things out of the apartment upstairs without disturbing Anita. So she tried to drug Anita and something went wrong."

"That's a hell of a theory," Mason said.

"Try and get one that fits the case any better," Drake told him. "One thing is certain—Fay Allison was living up there in apartment seven-oh-two. As far as Dane Grover is concerned, that's the thing that will make him throw everything overboard. He's a sensitive chap, from a good family. He doesn't like having his picture in the papers. Neither does his family."

"What about Clements?"

"Successful businessman, broker, speculator, lots of dough, domestic troubles, a wife who was trying to hook him for a bigger property settlement than Clements wanted to pay. Clements has a big apartment he leases by the year, where he lives officially. This place was a playhouse. Only a few people knew he had it. His wife would have given a lot of money to have found out about it."

"What's the wife doing now?"

"Sitting pretty. They don't know yet whether Clements left a will, but she has her community property rights, and Clements' books will be open for inspection now. He'd been juggling things around pretty much, and now a lot of stuff is going to come out—safety deposit boxes and things of that sort."

"How about the four people who met us in the hall?"

"I have all the stuff on them here. The men were Richard P. Nolin, a sort of partner in some of Clements' business, Manley L. Ogden, an income tax specialist, Don B. Ralston, who acted as dummy for Clements in some business transactions, and Vera Payson, who is someone's girl friend, but I'm damned if I can find out whose. Anyhow, those people knew of the hideout apartment and would go up there occasionally for a poker game. Last night as soon as the dame across the hall said Clements had company, they knew what that meant and went away. That's the story. The newspapers are lapping it up. Dane Grover isn't going to stay put much longer. You can't blame him. Pressure's getting pretty strong. All he has is Fay Allison's tearful denial. Louise Marlow says we have to do something fast."

Mason said, "Tragg thinks I had Carver Clements' key."

"Didn't you?"

"No."

"Where *did* you get it?"

Mason shook his head.

"Well," Drake said, "Carver Clements didn't have a key."

Mason nodded. "That is the only break we have in the case, Paul. We know Clements' key is missing. No one else does, because Tragg won't believe me when I tell him Clements hadn't given me his key."

Drake said, "It won't take Tragg long to figure the answer to that one. If Clements didn't give you the key, there's only one other person who could have given it to you."

Mason said, "We won't speculate too much on that, Paul."

"I gathered we wouldn't," Drake said dryly. "Remember this, Perry, you're representing a girl who's going to be faced with a murder rap. You may be able to beat that rap. It's circumstantial evidence. But in doing it, you'll have to think up some explanation that will satisfy an embarrassed lover who's being pitied by his friends, laughed at by his enemies, and ridiculed by the public."

Mason nodded.

"Whatever explanation you're going to make has to be made fast," Drake said. "My best guess is this Grover guy isn't going to stand the gaff much longer."

Mason said, "We'll push things to a quick hearing in court on a preliminary examination. In the meantime, Paul, find out everything you can about Carver Clements' background. Pay particular attention to Clements' wife. See if there isn't a man in her life. If she had known all along about that apartment . . ."

Drake shook his head dubiously. "I'll give it a once-over, Perry, but if she'd even known about that apartment, that would have been all she needed. If she could have raided that apartment with a photographer and had the deadwood on Carver Clements, she'd have boosted her property settlement another hundred grand and walked out smiling. She wouldn't have needed to use any poison."

Mason's strong, capable fingers were drumming gently on the edge of the desk. "There has to be *some* explanation, Paul."

Drake heaved himself wearily to his feet. "That's right," he said without enthusiasm, "and Tragg thinks he has it."

CHAPTER SEVEN

DELLA STREET, her eyes sparkling, entered Mason's private office from the door which led from the reception room and said, *"He's* here, chief."

"Who's here?" Mason asked, frowning.

She laughed. "Don't be like that. As far as this office is concerned, there is only one *he."*

"Dane Grover?"

"That's right."

"What sort?"

"Tall, sensitive-looking. Wavy, dark-brown hair, romantic eyes, with something of the poet about him. He's terribly crushed, of course. You can see he's dying ten thousand deaths every time he meets one of his friends. Gertie, at the switchboard, can't take her eyes off him."

Mason grinned and said, "Let's get him in, then, before Gertie either breaks up a romance or dies of unrequited love."

Della Street went out and returned after a few moments, ushering Dane Grover into the office.

Mason shook hands, invited Grover to take a seat. Grover glanced dubiously at Della Street. Mason smiled. "She's my right hand, Grover, keeps notes for me, and her thoughts to herself."

Grover said, "I suppose I'm unduly sensitive, but I can't stand it when people patronize me or snub me or pity me."

Mason nodded.

"I've had them do all three ever since the papers came out this morning."

Again Mason's answer was merely a nod.

"But," Grover went on, "I want you to know that I'll stick."

Mason thought that over for a moment, then held Grover's eyes. "For how long?"

"All the way."

"No matter *what* the evidence shows?"

Grover said, "The *evidence* shows the woman I love was living with Carver Clements as his mistress. The evidence simply can't be right. I love her, and I'm going to stick. I want you to tell her that, and I want you to know that. What you're going to have to do is going to take money. I want it to take *lots* of money. I don't want to leave any stone unturned. I'm here to see that you have what money you need—all you want, in fact."

"That's fine," Mason said. "Primarily, what I need is a little moral support. I want to be able to tell Fay Allison that you're sticking, and I want some facts."

"What facts?"

"How long have you been going with Fay Allison?"

"A matter of three or four months. Before then I was . . . well, sort of squiring both of the girls around."

"You mean Anita Bonsal?"

"Yes. I met Anita first. I went with her for a while. Then I went with both. Then I began to gravitate toward Fay Allison. I thought I was just making dates. Actually I was falling in love."

"And Anita?"

"She's like a sister to both of us. She's been simply grand in this whole thing. She's promised me that she'll do everything she can do."

"Could Fay Allison have been living with Carver Clements?"

"She had the physical opportunity, if that's what you mean."

"You didn't see her every night?"

"No."

"What does Anita say?"

"Anita says the charge is ridiculous, absolutely absurd."

"Do you know of any place where Fay Allison could have had access to cyanide of potassium?"

"That's what I wanted to tell you about, Mr. Mason."

"Go ahead."

"Out at my place the gardener uses it. I don't know just what for, but . . . well, out there the other day, when he was showing Fay around the place . . ."

"Yes, yes," Mason said impatiently as Grover paused, "go on."

"Well, I know the gardener was explaining to her something about it. He told her to be very careful not to touch that sack because it contained cyanide, and I remember she asked him a few questions about what he used it for, but I wasn't paying much attention. It's the basis of some sort of a spray, and then I believe it's used for the plants."

"Who else was present?"

"Just the three of us."

"Has your gardener read the papers?"

Grover nodded.

"Can you trust him?"

"With my life. He's very devoted to me. He's been with us for twenty years."

"What's his name?"

"Barney Sheff. My mother took an interest in him and . . . well, rehabilitated him."

"He'd been in trouble?"

"Yes"

"In the pen?"

"That's right."

"Then what?"

"Then he was released. He had a chance to get parole if he could get a job. Mother gave him the job. He's been terribly devoted ever since."

"You have a hothouse?"

"Yes."

"I'm wondering if you have fully explored the possibilities of orchid growing."

"We're not interested in orchid growing. We can buy them and—"

"I wonder," Mason said in exactly the same tone and with the same spacing of words, "if you have fully investigated the possibilities of growing orchids."

"I tell you we . . ."

"Fully investigated the possibilities of growing orchids," Mason said again.

"You mean . . . oh, you mean we should send Barney Sheff to . . ."

"Fully investigate the possibilities of growing orchids."

Dane Grover studied Mason silently for a few seconds. Then abruptly he arose from the chair, extended his hand, and said, "I brought you some money. I thought you might need it."

He carelessly tossed an envelope on the desk.

"How about your mother?" Mason asked.

Grover touched his tongue to dry lips, then clamped his mouth in a straight line. "Mother," he said, "is naturally embarrassed. I don't think *her* feelings need to enter into it."

And with that he marched out of the office.

Mason reached for the envelope Grover had tossed on his desk. It was well filled with hundred-dollar bills.

Della Street came over to take the money. "When I get so interested in a man," she said, "that I neglect to count the money, you know I'm becoming incurably romantic. How much, chief?"

"Plenty," Mason said.

Della Street was counting it when the unlisted telephone on her desk rang stridently.

She picked up the receiver and heard Drake's voice on the line.

"Hi, Paul," she said.

"Hi, Della. Perry there?"

"Yes."

"Okay," Drake said wearily, "I'm making a progress report. Tell him Lieutenant Tragg nabbed the Grover gardener, a chap by the name of Sheff. They're holding him as a material witness, seem to be all worked up about what they've discovered. Can't find out what it is. Caroline Manning Grover."

Della Street sat motionless at the desk, holding the receiver.

"Hello, hello," Drake said. "Are you there?"

"I'm here," Della said. "I'll tell him." She hung up the phone.

CHAPTER EIGHT

It was after nine o'clock that night when Della Street, signing the register in the elevator, was whisked up to the fl or where Perry Mason had his offices.

The offices of the Drake Detective Agency on the

same floor, nearer the elevator, were kept open twenty-four hours a day. The innocent-looking entrance door showed merely a single oblong of frosted glass, the illumination back of the glass showing the offices were open, but giving no indication of the unceasing nocturnal activities of the staff which worked in a veritable rabbit warren of offices.

Della Street started to look in on Paul Drake, then changed her mind and kept on walking down the long, dark corridor, the rapid tempo of her heels echoing back at her from the night silence of the door-lined hallway.

She rounded the elbow in the corridor and saw that lights were on in Mason's office. She fitted her latchkey to the outer door, crossed through the entrance office, and opened the door of Mason's private office.

The lawyer was pacing the floor, thumbs pushed in the armholes of his best, head shoved forward, wrapped in such concentration that he did not even notice the opening of the door.

The desk was littered with photographs. There were numerous sheets of the flimsy which Paul Drake used in making reports to clients.

Della stood quietly in the doorway, watching the tall, lean-waisted man pacing back and forth. He was granite-hard of face, broad-shouldered, flat-stomached; the seething action of his restless mind demanded physical outlet in order to preserve some semblance of internal balance, and this restless pacing was but an unconscious reflex.

After almost a minute Della Street said, "Hello, chief. Can I help?"

Mason looked up at her with a start. "What are you doing here?"

"I came up to see if you were working and, if so, if there was anything I could do to help."

He smiled. "I'm not working. I'm like an animal running around his cage trying to find an outlet."

"Had any dinner?" she asked.

He glanced at his wristwatch and said, "Not yet."

"What time is it?" Della Street asked.

He had to look at his wristwatch again in order to tell her. "Nine-forty."

She laughed. "I knew you didn't even look the first time you went through the motions. Come on, chief, you've got to go get something to eat. The case will still be here when you get back."

"How do we know it will?" Mason said. "I've been talking with Louise Marlow on the phone. She's been in touch with Dane Grover and she knows Dane Grover's mother. Dane Grover says he'll stick. How does *he* know what he'll do? He's exploring uncharted depths in his own mind. He doesn't know what he'll find. His friends and relatives are turning the knife in the wound with their sympathy, the silent accusation of their every glance. How the hell does he know what he's going to do? How can he tell whether he'll stick?"

"Just the same," Della Street insisted, "*I* think he'll do it. It's through situations such as this that character is created."

"You're just talking to keep your courage up," Mason said. "I've pulled that line with a jury once or twice myself. Soul-seared in a crucible of adversity—the tempering fires of fate—burning away the fat of wealthy complacency as he comes to grips with the fundamentals of life—baloney!"

She smiled faintly.

"The guy's undergoing the tortures of the damned," Mason went on. "He can't help but be influenced by the evidence, by the worldly-wise, cynical skepticism of all his associates. The woman he loves on the night before the wedding having trouble trying to push herself away from the slimy embraces of the man who gave her money and a certain measure of security—until she had an opportunity to trade that security in on a newer and better model."

"Chief, you simply *have* to eat."

Mason walked over to the desk. "Look at 'em," he

said. "Photographs! And Drake had the devil's own time obtaining them—copies of the police photographs—the body on the floor, glass on the table, an overturned chair, a newspaper half open by a reading chair, an ordinary, mediocre apartment as drab as the sordid affair for which it was used. And somewhere in those photographs I've got to find the clue that will establish the innocence of a woman, not only innocence of the crime of murder, but innocence of the crime of betraying the man she loved."

Mason crossed over to the desk, picked up the magnifying glass which was on his blotter, started once more examining the pictures. "And, hang it, Della," he said, "I think the thing's here somewhere. That glass on the table, a little Scotch and soda in the bottom, Fay Allison's fingerprints all over it. Then there's the brazen touch of that crimson kiss on the forehead."

"Indicating a woman was with him just before he died?"

"Not necessarily. That lipstick is a perfect imprint of a pair of lips. There was no lipstick on his lips, just there on the forehead. A shrewd man could well have smeared lipstick on his lips, pressed them against Clements' forehead after the poison had taken effect, and so directed suspicion away from himself. This could well have happened if the man had known some woman was in the habit of visiting Clements there in that apartment.

"It's a clue that so obviously indicates a woman that I find myself getting suspicious of it. If there were only something to give me a starting point. If we only had a little more time."

Della Street walked over to the desk. The cool tips of her fingers slid over Mason's eyes. She said, "Stop it. Come and get something to eat. Let's talk it over . . ."

"Haven't you had dinner?"

She smiled and shook her head. "I knew you'd be working and that if someone didn't rescue you, you'd be pacing the floor until two or three o'clock in the morning. What's Paul Drake found out?"

She picked up the sheets of flimsy, placed them together, folded them, stacked up the photographs, put the flimsy on top of the photographs, and anchored everything in place with a paperweight. "Come on, chief, I'm famished."

Mason walked over to the coat closet. Della had to stand on tiptoes to help him with his topcoat. The lawyer took his hat, switched out lights, and walked down the corridor with Della Street.

But he didn't really answer her question until after he had become relaxed in one of the booths in their favorite restaurant. Then he pushed back the plates containing the wreckage of a thick steak, shoestring potatoes, golden-brown toasted and buttered French bread, and a lettuce and tomato salad.

He poured more coffee, then said, "Drake hasn't found out much, just background."

"What, for instance?" Della Street asked.

Mason said wearily, "It's the same old seven and six. The wife, Marline Austin Clements, apparently was swept off her feet by Carver Clements' determination to get her, by the sheer power of the man.

"She overlooked the fact that after he had her safely listed as one of his legal chattels, with title in good order, he used that same acquisitive, aggressive tenacity of purpose to get other things he wanted. Marline was left pretty much alone. That's the price one has to pay for marrying men of that type."

"And so?" Della asked.

"And so," Mason said, "in the course of time, Carver Clements turned to other interests. Hang it, Della, we have one thing to work on, only one thing, the fact that Clements had no key on his body.

"You remember the four people who met us in the corridor. They had to get in that apartment house some way. Remember the outer door was locked. Any of the tenants could release the latch by pressing the button of an electric release. But if the tenant of some apartment didn't press the release button, it was necessary for any visitor to have a key in order to get in.

"Now then, those four people got in. How? They must have had a key. Regardless of what they now say, one of them must have had a key."

"The missing key?" Della asked.

"That's what we have to find out."

"What story did they give the police?"

"I don't know. The police have them sewed up tight. I've got to get one of them on the stand and cross-examine him. Then we'll at least have something to go on."

"So we have to try for an immediate hearing and then go it blind?"

"That's about the size of it."

"Was that key in Fay Allison's purse Carver Clements' missing key?"

"It *could* have been. If so, either Fay was playing house or the key was planted. In that case when was it planted, how, and by whom? I'm inclined to think Clements' key must have been on his body at the time he was murdered. It wasn't there when the police arrived. That's the one really significant clue we have to work on."

Della Street shook her head. "It's too deep for me, but I guess you're going to have to wade into it. I can tell you one thing. Louise Marlow is a brick. I've known her since I was a child. If there's anything she can do to help, you can count on her."

Mason lit a cigarette. "Ordinarily I'd spar for time, but in this case I'm afraid time is our enemy, Della. We're going to have to walk into court with all the assurance in the world and pull a very large rabbit out of a very small hat."

She smiled. "Where do we get the rabbit?"

"Back in the office," he said, "studying those photographs, looking for a clue, and . . ." Suddenly he snapped to startled attention.

"What is it, chief?"

"I was just thinking. The glass on the table in seven-oh-two, there was a little whiskey and soda in the bottom of it, just a spoonful or two."

"Well?" she asked.

"What happens when you drink Scotch and soda, Della?"

"Why . . . you always have a little. It sticks to the side of the glass and then gradually settles back."

Mason shook his head. His eyes were glowing now. "You leave ice cubes in the glass," he said, "and then after a while they melt and leave an inch or so of water."

She matched his excitement. "Then there was no ice in the woman's glass?"

"And none in Carver Clements'. Yet there was a thermos jar of ice cubes on the table. Come on, Della, we're going back and *really* study those photographs!"

CHAPTER NINE

JUDGE RANDOLPH JORDAN ascended the bench and rapped the court to order.

"People versus Fay Allison."

"Ready for the defendant," Mason said.

"Ready for the prosecution," Stewart Linn announced.

Linn, one of the best of the trial deputies in the district attorney's office, was a thin-faced, steely-eyed, cautious individual who had the mind of an accountant, an encyclopedic knowledge of law, and the cold-blooded mercilessness of a steel trap.

Linn was under no illusions as to the resourcefulness of his adversary, and he had all the caution of a boxer approaching a heavyweight champion.

"Call Dr. Charles Keene," he said.

Dr. Keene came forward, qualified himself as a physician and surgeon who had had great experience in medical necropsies, particularly in cases of homicide.

"On the tenth of this month did you have occasion to

examine a body in apartment seven-oh-two at the Mandrake Arms?"

"I did."

"What time was it?"

"It was about two o'clock in the morning."

"What did you find?"

"I found the body of a man of approximately fifty-two years of age, fairly well-fleshed, quite bald, but otherwise very well preserved for a man of his age. The body was lying on the floor, sprawled forward, head toward the door, feet toward the interior of the apartment, the left arm doubled up and lying under him, the right arm flung out, the left side of the face resting on the carpet. The man had been dead for several hours. I fix the time of death as having been during a period between seven o'clock and nine o'clock that evening. I cannot place the time of death any closer than that, but I will swear that it was within those time limits."

"And did you determine the cause of death?"

"Not at that time. I did later."

"What was the cause of death?"

"Poisoning caused by the ingestion of cyanide of potassium."

"Did you notice anything about the physical appearance of the man's body?"

"You mean with reference to lipstick?"

"Yes."

"There was a red smear on the upper part of the forehead, apparently caused by lips that had been heavily coated with lipstick and then pressed against the skin in a somewhat puckered condition."

"You mean the skin was puckered?"

"No," Dr. Linn said, smiling. "I mean the lips were puckered. It was as though some woman had administered a last kiss. The lipstick was deposited at the upper part of the forehead, where the skin across the scalp was stretched tight and smooth. It would have been above the hairline of an individual who was not bald."

"Cross-examine," Linn announced.

"No questions," Mason said.

"Call Benjamin Harlan," Linn said.

Benjamin Harlan, a huge, lumbering giant of a man, took the stand with a good-natured smile, promptly proceeded to qualify himself as a fingerprint and indentification expert of some twenty years' experience.

Stewart Linn, by skillful, adroit questions, led him through an account of his activities on the date in question, the finding of the body, the dusting of various things in the apartment, the finding of no latent fingerprints on the glass which the prosecution referred to as the "murder glass," indicating this glass had been wiped clean of prints, the finding of prints on the glass on the table which the prosecution referred to as the "decoy glass," on the toothbrush, on the tube of toothpaste, and various other articles. These latent fingerprints had coincided with the rolled fingerprints taken from the hands of Fay Allison, the defendant in the case.

Harlan also identified a whole series of photographs taken by the police showing the position of the body when it was discovered, the furnishings in the apartment, the table, the overturned chair, the so-called murder glass which had rolled along the floor, the so-called decoy glass on the table, which bore unmistakably the fresh fingerprints of Fay Allison, the bottle of Scotch whiskey, the bottle of soda water, the thermos jar containing ice cubes.

"Cross-examine," Linn said triumphantly.

Mason said, "You have had some twenty years' experience as a fingerprint expert, Mr. Harlan?"

"That's right."

"And an identification expert?"

"Yes, sir."

"Now, you have heard Dr. Keene's testimony about the lipstick on the forehead of the dead man?"

"Yes, sir."

"And that lipstick, I believe, shows in this photograph which I now hand you?"

"Yes, sir. Not only that, but I have a close-up of that lipstick stain which I myself took with one of the cameras I use for close-up photography. I have an enlargement of that negative, in case you're interested."

"I'm very much interested," Mason said. "Will you produce the enlargement, please?"

Harlan produced the photograph from his briefcase, showing a section of the forehead of the dead man, with the stain of lips outlined clearly and in microscopic detail.

"What is the scale of this photograph?" Mason asked.

"Life size," Harlan said. "I have a standard of distances by which I can take photographs to a scale of exactly life size."

"Thank you," Mason said. "I'd like to have this photograph received in evidence."

"No objection," Linn said.

"And it is, is it not, a matter of fact that the little lines shown in this photograph are fully as distinctive as the ridges and whorls of a fingerprint?"

"Just what do you mean?"

"Isn't it a fact well known to identification experts that the little wrinkles which form in a person's lips are fully as individual as the lines of a fingerprint?"

"It's not a 'well-known' fact."

"But it *is* a fact?"

"Yes, sir, it is."

"So that by measuring the distance between the little lines which are shown on this photograph, indicating the pucker lines of the skin, it would be fully possible to identify the lips which made this lipstick print as it would be to identify a person who had left a fingerprint upon the scalp of the dead man."

"Yes, sir."

"Now, you have testified to having made rolled imprints of the defendant's fingers and compared those with the fingerprints found on the glass."

"Yes, sir."

"Have you made any attempt to take an imprint of her

lips and compare that print with the print of the lipstick on the forehead of the decedent?"

"No, sir," Harlan said, shifting his position uneasily.

"Why not?"

"Well, in the first place, Mr. Mason, the fact that the pucker lines of lips are so highly individualized is not a generally known fact."....

"But *you* know it."

"Yes, sir."

"And the more skilled experts in your profession know it?"

"Yes, sir."

"Why didn't you do it then?"

Harlan shifted his position again, crossed his legs, glanced somewhat helplessly at Stewart Linn, the deputy prosecutor.

"Oh, if the Court please," Linn said, promptly taking his cue from that glance, "this hardly seems to be cross-examination. The inquiry is wandering far afield. I will object to the question on the ground that it's incompetent, irrelevant and immaterial, and not proper cross-examination."

"Overruled," Judge Jordan snapped. "Answer the question!"

Harlan cleared his throat. "Well," he said, "I guess I just never thought of it."

"Think of it now," Mason said with a gesture that was a flourish. "Go ahead and take the imprint right now and right here. Put on plenty of lipstick, Miss Allison. Let's see how your lips compare with those on the dead man's forehead."

"Oh, if the Court please," Linn said wearily, "this hardly seems to be cross-examination. If Mr. Mason wants to make Harlan his own witness and call for this test as a part of the defendant's case, that will be one thing, but this certainly isn't cross-examination."

"It may be cross-examination of Harlan's qualifications as an expert," Judge Jordan ruled.

With faint sarcasm Linn said, "Isn't that stretching a technicality rather far?"

"Your objection was highly technical," Judge Jordan snapped. "It is overruled, and my ruling will stand. Take the impression, Mr. Harlan."

Fay Allison, with trembling hands, daubed lipstick heavily on her mouth. Then, using the makeup mirror in her purse, smoothed off the lipstick with the tip of her little finger.

"Go ahead," Mason said to Harlan, "check on her lips."

Harlan, taking a piece of white paper from his briefcase, moved down to where the defendant was sitting beside Perry Mason and pressed the white paper against her lips. He removed the paper and examined the imprint.

"Go ahead," Mason said to Harlan, "make your comparison and announce the result to the Court."

Harlan said, "Of course, I have not the facilities here for making a miscroscopic comparison, but I can tell from even a superficial examination of the lip lines that these lips did not make that print."

"Thank you," Mason said. "That's all."

Judge Jordan was interested. "These lines appear in the lips only when the lips are puckered, as in giving a kiss?"

"No, Your Honor, they are in the lips all the time, as an examination will show, but when the lips are puckered, the lines are intensified."

"And these lip markings are different with each individual?"

"Yes, Your Honor."

"So that you are now prepared to state to the Court that despite the fingerprints of the defendant on the glass and other objects, her lips definitely could not have left the imprint on the dead man's forehead?"

"Yes, Your Honor."

"That's all," Judge Jordan said.

"Of course," Linn pointed out, "the fact that the defendant did not leave that kiss imprint on the man's forehead doesn't necessarily mean a thing, Your Honor. In fact, he may have met his death *because* the defendant found that lipstick on his forehead. The evidence of the fingerprints is quite conclusive that the defendant was in that apartment."

"The Court understands the evidence. Proceed with your case," Judge Jordan said.

"Furthermore," Linn went on angrily, "I will now show the Court that there was every possibility the print of that lipstick could have been deliberately planted by none other than the attorney for the defendant and his charming and very efficient secretary. I will proceed to prove that by calling Don B. Ralston to the stand."

Ralston came forward and took the stand, his manner that of a man who wishes very much he were many miles away.

"Your name is Don B. Ralston? You reside at Two-nine-three-five Creelmore Avenue in this city?"

"Yes, sir."

"And you knew Carver L. Clements in his lifetime?"

"Yes."

"Were rather intimately associated with him?"

"Yes, sir."

"In a business way?"

"Yes, sir."

"Now, on the night, or rather early in the morning, of the tenth of this month, did you have occasion to go to Carver L. Clements' apartment, being apartment number seven-oh-two in the Mandrake Arms Apartments in this city?"

"I did, yes, sir."

"What time was it?"

"Around . . . well, it was between one and two in the morning . . . I would say somewhere around one-thirty."

"Were you alone?"

"No, sir."

"Who was with you?"

"Richard P. Nolin, who is a business associate, or was a business associate of Mr. Clements; Manley L. Ogden, who handled some of Mr. Clements' income tax work; and a Miss Vera Payson, a friend of—well, a friend of all of us."

"What happened when you went to that apartment? Did you enter it?"

"No, sir."

"Tell us just what happened."

"Well, we left the elevator on the seventh floor, and as we were walking up the corridor, I noticed two people coming down the corridor toward us."

"Now, when you say 'down the corridor,' do you mean from the direction of apartment seven-oh-two?"

"That's right, yes, sir."

"And who were these people?"

"Mr. Perry Mason and his secretary, Miss Street."

"And did you actually enter the apartment of Carver Clements?"

"I did not."

"Why not?"

"When I got to the door of apartment seven-oh-two, I pushed the doorbell and heard the sound of the buzzer on the inside of the apartment. Almost instantly the door of an apartment across the hall opened, and a woman who seemed to be somewhat irritated complained that she had been unable to sleep because of people ringing the buzzer of that apartment, and stated in effect that other people were in there with Mr. Clements. So we left immediately."

"Now, then, Your Honor," Stewart Linn said, "I propose to show that the two people referred to by the person living in the apartment across the hallway were none other than Mr. Mason and Miss Street, who had actually entered that apartment and were closeted in there with the dead man and the evidence for an undetermined length of time."

"Go ahead and show it," Judge Jordan said.

"Just a moment," Mason said. "Before you do that, I want to cross-examine this witness."

"Cross-examine him, then."

"When you arrived at the Mandrake Arms, the door to the street was locked, was it not?"

"Yes, sir."

"What did you do?"

"We went up to the seventh floor and—"

"I understand that, but how did you get in? How did you get past the entrance door? You had a key, didn't you?"

"No, sir."

"Then how *did* you get in?"

"Why, *you* let us in."

"*I* did?"

"Yes."

"Understand," Mason said, "I am not now referring to the time you came up from the street in the custody of the police. I am now referring to the time when you first entered that apartment house on the morning of the tenth of this month—the first time you went in."

"Yes, sir. I understand. You let us in."

"What makes you say that?"

"Well, because you and your secretary were in Carver Clements' apartment, and—"

"You, yourself, don't *know* we were in there, do you?"

"Well, I surmise it. We met you just after you had left the apartment. You were hurrying down the hall toward the elevator."

Mason said, "I don't want your surmises. You don't even know I had been in that apartment. I want you to tell us how you got past the locked street door. No surmises now. Just how did you get in? Exactly what did you do?"

"We pressed the button of Carver Clements' apartment, and you—or at any rate someone—answered by pressing the button which released the electric door catch on the outer door. As soon as we heard the sound of buzzing, which indicated the lock was released, we pushed the door open and went in."

"Let's not have any misunderstanding about this," Mason said. "Who was it pushed the button of Carver Clements' apartment?"

"I did."

"I'm talking now about the button in front of the outer door of the apartment house."

"Yes, sir."

"And, having pressed that button, you waited until the buzzer announced the door was being opened?"

"Yes, sir."

"How long?"

"Not over a second or two."

Mason said to the witness, "One more question: did you go right up after you entered the apartment house?"

"We . . . no, sir, not *right* away. We stopped for a few moments there in the lobby to talk about the type of poker we wanted to play. Miss Payson had lost some money on one of these wild poker games where the dealer has the opportunity of calling any kind of game he wants, some of them having the one-eyed jacks wild, and others having seven cards from which five are selected, and things of that sort."

"How long were you talking?"

"Oh, a couple of minutes, perhaps."

"And you decided on the type of poker you wanted to play?"

"Yes."

"And then went right up?"

"Yes."

"Where was the elevator?"

"The elevator was . . . now, wait a minute, I don't remember exactly. It was on one of the upper floors. I remember we pressed the button and it took it a little while to come down to where we were."

"That's all," Mason said.

Della Street's fingers dug into his arm. "Aren't you going to ask him about the key?" she whispered.

"Not yet," Mason said, a light of triumph in his eyes. "I know what happened now, Della. Give us the breaks and we've got this case in the bag. First, make him prove we were in that apartment."

Linn said, "I will now call Miss Shirley Tanner to the stand."

The young woman who advanced to the stand was very different from the disheveled, sleepless, and nervous individual who had been so angry at the time Mason and Della Street had pressed the button of apartment 702.

"Your name is Shirley Tanner, and you reside in apartment seven-oh-one of the Mandrake Arms Apartments in this city?"

"Yes, sir."

"And have for how long?"

She smiled and said, "Not very long. I put in three weeks apartment hunting and finally secured a sublease on apartment seven-oh-one on the afternoon of the eighth. I moved in on the ninth, which explains why I was tired almost to the point of having hysterics."

"You had difficulty sleeping?"

"Yes."

"And on the morning of the tenth did you have any experiences which annoyed you—that is, experiences in connection with the ringing of the buzzer in the apartment next door?"

"I most certainly did, yes, sir."

"Tell us exactly what happened."

"I had been taking sleeping medicine from time to time, but for some reason or other this night I was so nervous the sleeping medicine didn't do me any good. I had been moving and unpacking, and my nerves were all keyed up. I was physically and mentally exhausted. I tried to sleep, but I was too tired. I guess perhaps you know how it is, Your Honor," she said, turning to the judge with a winsome smile.

The judge regarded the attractive young woman, smiled in a fatherly way, nodded, and said, "We all get overtired at times. Go on with your testimony, Miss Tanner."

"Well, I think I had just gotten to sleep when I was awakened by a continual sounding of the buzzer over there in the apartment across the hall. It was a low, persistent noise which became exceedingly irritating to a person in my nervous state, who was trying to sleep."

"Go on," Linn said. "What did you do?"

"I finally got up and put on a robe and went to the door and flung it open. I was terribly angry at the very idea of people making so much noise at that hour of the morning. You see, those apartments aren't too soundproof and there is a ventilating system over the doors of the apartments. The one over the door of seven-oh-two was apparently open, and I had left mine open for nighttime ventilation. And then I was angry at myself for getting so upset over the noise. I knew my allowing myself to get so angry would prevent me from sleeping at all, which is why I lay still for what seemed an interminable time before I opened the door."

Linn smiled. "So you became angry at the people in the hallway and then became angry at yourself for being angry?"

Her laugh was musical. "That's about the way it happened."

"And you say you *flung* open the door?"

"Yes, sir."

"What did you find?"

"Two people across the hall."

"Did you recognize them?"

"I didn't know them at the time, but I know them now."

"Who were they?"

She pointed a dramatic finger at Perry Mason.

"Mr. Perry Mason, the lawyer for the defendant, and the young woman, I believe his secretary, who is sitting there beside him—not the defendant, but the woman on the other side."

"Miss Della Street," Mason said with a bow.

"Thank you," she said.

"And," Linn went on, "what did you see those people do?"

She said, "I saw them enter the apartment."

"Did you see how they entered the apartment . . . I mean, how did they get the door open?"

"They must have used a key. Mr. Mason was just pushing the door open and I—"

"No surmises, please," Linn broke in. "Did you actually *see* Mr. Mason using a key?"

"Well, I heard him."

"What do you mean?"

"As I was opening my door I heard metal rasping against metal, the way a key does when it scrapes against a lock. And then when I had my door all the way open, I saw Mr. Mason pushing his way into seven-oh-two."

"But you only know he must have had a key because you heard the sound of metal rubbing against metal?"

"Well, it stands to reason . . ."

"But you only heard the sound of metal against metal?"

"Yes, and the click of the lock."

"Did you say anything to Mr. Mason and Miss Street?"

"I most certainly did, and then I slammed the door and went back to bed. But I was so mad by that time I simply couldn't close my eyes and keep them closed. I couldn't understand why, if a person had a key, he would go through all that agony of ringing a doorbell and waking me up. Why didn't they simply go in there in the first place and—"

"Now, never mind that," Linn interrupted impatiently, holding up his hand palm outward and moving it back and forth as though patting the words back into her mouth. "Never mind your conclusions, never mind your reasons. Just tell the Court what you *saw*."

"Yes, sir."

"What happened after that?"

"After that, when I was trying to sleep—I would say just a few seconds after that—I heard that buzzer again. And this time I was *good* and mad."

"And what did you do?"

"I swung open the door and started to give these people a piece of my mind."

"People?" Linn prompted.

"There were four people standing there. The Mr. Ralston who had just testified, two other men, and a woman. They were standing there at the doorway, jabbing away at the button, and I told them this was a sweet time to be calling on someone and making a racket and that anyway the gentleman already had company, so if he didn't answer his door, it was because he didn't want to."

"Did you at that time see Mr. Mason and Miss Street walking down the corridor?"

"No, I did not. I had my door open only far enough to show me the door of apartment seven-oh-two across the way. You see, my door opens toward the end of the corridor away from the elevator. My apartment is a corner apartment and seven-oh-two is a corner apartment. So, when my door is open, I can only see just that blind end of the corridor unless I open it all the way."

"Thank you," Linn said. "Now you distinctly saw Mr. Mason and Miss Street enter that apartment?"

"Yes."

"And close the door behind them?"

"Yes."

"Cross-examine!" Linn said triumphantly.

Mason, taking a notebook from his pocket, walked up to stand beside Shirley Tanner, but his voice was good-natured. "Miss Tanner," he said, "are you certain that you heard me rub metal against the keyhole of that door?"

"Certain," she said.

"My back was toward you?"

"It was when I first opened my door, yes. I saw your

face, however, just after you went in the door. You turned around and looked at me over your shoulder."

"Oh, we'll stipulate," Linn said with an exaggerated note of weariness in his voice, "that the witness couldn't see through Mr. Mason's back. Perhaps learned counsel was carrying the key in his teeth."

"Thank you," Mason said, turning toward Linn. Then suddenly stepping forward, he clapped his notebook against Shirley Tanner's face.

The witness screamed and jumped back.

Linn was on his feet. "What are you trying to do," he shouted, "intimidate the witness?"

Judge Jordan pounded with his gavel. "Mr. Mason!" he reprimanded. "That is contempt of court!"

Mason said, "Please let me explain, Your Honor. The Prosecution took the lip prints of my client. I feel that I am entitled to take the lip prints of this witness. I will cheerfully admit to being in contempt of court, in the event I am wrong, but I would like to extend this imprint of Shirley Tanner's lips to Mr. Benjamin Harlan, the identification expert, and ask him whether or not the print made by these lips is not the same as that of the lipstick kiss which was found on the forehead of the deceased, Carver L. Clements."

There was a tense, dramatic silence in the courtroom.

Mason stepped forward and handed the notebook to Benjamin Harlan.

From the witness stand came a shrill scream of terror. Shirley Tanner tried to get to her feet, her eyes fastened on Mason, wide, round, and terrified, her face the color of putty beneath the makeup which suddenly showed as dabbed-on bits of orange.

She couldn't make it. Her knees buckled. She tried to catch herself, then fell to the floor.

CHAPTER TEN

IT WAS when order was restored in the courtroom that Perry Mason exploded his second bombshell.

"Your Honor," he said, "either Fay Allison is innocent or she is guilty. If she is innocent, someone framed the evidence which would discredit her. And if someone did frame that evidence, there is only one person who could have done it, one person who could have had access to the defendant's apartment, one person who could have transported glasses, toothbrushes, and toothpaste containing Fay Allison's fingerprints, one person who could have transported clothes bearing the unmistakable stamp of ownership of the defendant in this case.

"Your Honor, I request that Anita Bonsal be called to the stand."

There was a moment's sudden and dramatic silence.

Anita Bonsal, there in the courtroom, felt suddenly as though she had been stripped stark naked by one swift gesture.

One moment she had been sitting there completely lost in the proceedings, trying to adjust her mind to what was happening, attempting to keep pace with the swift rush of developments. The next moment everyone in the courtroom was seeking her out with staring, prying eyes.

It was as though she had been quietly bathing and the side of the building had collapsed and left her naked and exposed to the curious eyes of the multitude.

In that sudden surge of panic, Anita did the worst thing she could possibly have done. She ran.

They were after her then, a throng of humanity, actuated only by the mass instinct to pursue that which ran for cover.

Elevators were too slow for Anita's frantic feet. Behind her was the bedlam of the crowd, a babble of voices which speedily grew into a roar.

Anita dashed to the stairs, went scrambling down them,

and found herself in another hallway in the Hall of Justice. She dashed the length of that hallway, frantically trying to find the stairs. She could not find them.

An elevator offered her welcome haven. It was standing with the doors open, the red light on above it.

"Going down," the attendant said.

Anita fairly flung herself into the cage.

"What's the hurry?" the attendant asked.

Shreds of reason were beginning to return to Anita's fear-racked mind.

"They're calling my case," she said. "Let me off at . . ."

"I know," the man said, smiling. "Third floor. Domestic Relations Court."

He slid the cage to a smooth stop at the third floor. "Out to the left," he said. "Department Twelve."

Anita's mind was beginning to work now, functioning smoothly, cunningly.

She smiled her thanks to the elevator attendant, walked rapidly to the left, pushed open the door of Department 12 of the Superior Court, and entered the partially filled courtroom with all the assurance of a witness coming to testify in a case.

She marched down the center aisle, gave an apologetic smile to the young woman who was in the aisle seat, then crossed in front of her and calmly seated herself in the middle seat in the row of benches.

She was now wrapped in anonymity. Only her breathlessness and the pounding of her pulses gave indication that she was the quarry for which the crowd was searching.

Then slowly the triumphant smile faded from her face. The realization of what was bound to be the effect of what she had done stabbed her consciousness. She had admitted her guilt. She could flee now to the farthest corners of the earth, but her guilt would always follow her. She would always be an object of scorn and contempt.

Perry Mason had shown that she had not killed Carver Clements, but he had also shown that she had done something which in the minds of all men would be even worse. She had betrayed her friendship. She had tried to besmirch Fay Allison's reputation. She had attempted the murder of her own roommate by giving her an overdose of sleeping tablets.

How much would Mason have been able to prove? She had no way of knowing. The man was uncanny with his shrewdness of perception. But there was no need for him to prove now. Her flight had given Mason all the proof he needed.

She must disappear, and that would not be easy. By evening her photograph would be emblazoned upon the pages of every newspaper in the city.

CHAPTER ELEVEN

BACK in the courtroom, all but deserted now except for the county officials who were crowding around Shirley Tanner, Mason was asking questions in a low voice.

There was no more stamina left in Shirley Tanner. She heard her own voice answering the persistent drone of Mason's searching questions.

"You knew that Clements had this apartment in seven-oh-two? You deliberately made such a high offer that you were able to sublease apartment seven-oh-one? You were suspicious of Clements and wanted to spy on him?"

"Yes," Shirley said, and her voice was all but inaudible to her own ears, although her eyes told her that the court reporter, standing beside her with his hand moving unobtrusively over his notebook, was taking down all that was said.

"You were furious when you realized that Carver Clements had *another* mistress, that all his talk to you about waiting until he could get his divorce was merely another bait which you had grabbed."

Again she said, "Yes." It seemed the easiest thing to

Gideon's Art, the highly acclaimed new thriller by J. J. Marric (John Creasey) and selections by other
Gordon Ashe
A. A. Fair
the supply lasts, send the card to get your 12 mysteries.
First Class
Permit No. 7
Roslyn, N.Y.
Business Reply Mail
No postage stamp necessary if mailed in the United States
Postage Will Be Paid By
The Detective Book Club
Roslyn, New York 11576
How to make crime pay: use this card to get away with $61.95 worth of mystery books for $1.
(See other side for further details.)

say, the only thing that she could say. There was no strength in her any more to think up lies.

"You made the mistake of loving him," Mason said. "It wasn't his money *you* were after, and you administered the poison. How did you do it, Shirley?"

She said, "I'd poisoned the drink I held in my hand. I knew it made Carver furious when I drank because whiskey makes me lose control of myself, and he never knew what I was going to do when I was drunk.

"I rang his bell, holding that glass in my hand. I leered at him tipsily when he opened the door, and walked on in. I said, 'Hello, Carver darling. Meet your next-door neighbor,' and I raised the glass to my lips.

"He reacted just as I knew he would. He was furious. He said, 'You little devil, what're you doing here? I've told you I'll do the drinking for both of us.' He snatched the glass from me and drained it."

"What happened?" Mason asked.

"For a moment, nothing," she said. "He went back to the chair and sat down. I leaned over him and pressed that kiss on his head. It was a good-by kiss. He looked at me, frowned, suddenly jumped to his feet, and tried to run to the door. Then he staggered and fell face forward."

"And what did you do?"

"I took the key to his apartment from his pocket so I could get back in to fix things the way I wanted and get possession of the glass, but I was afraid to be there while he was . . . retching and twisting . . . and dying."

Mason nodded. "You went back to your own apartment and then after you had waited a few minutes and thought it was safe to go back, you couldn't, because Anita Bonsal was at the door?"

Shirley Tanner nodded and said, "She had a key. She went in. I supposed, of course, she'd call the police and that they'd come at any time. I didn't dare to go in there then. I tried to sleep and couldn't. Finally I decided the police weren't coming after all. It was past midnight then."

"So then you went back in there? You were in there when Don Ralston rang the bell. You—"

"Yes," she said. "I went back into that apartment. By that time I had put on a bathrobe and pajamas and ruffled my hair all up. If anyone had said anything to me, if I had been caught, I had a story all prepared to tell them—that I had heard the door open and someone run down the corridor, that I had opened my door and found the door of seven-oh-two ajar, and I had just that minute looked in to see what had happened."

"All right," Mason said, "That was your story. What did you do?"

"I went across the hall. I went in and wiped all my fingerprints off that glass on the floor. Then the buzzer sounded from the street door."

"What did you do?"

"I saw someone had fixed up the evidence just the way I had been going to fix it up. A bottle of Scotch on the table, a bottle of soda, a pail of ice cubes."

"So what did you do?"

She said, "I pushed the button which released the downstairs door catch and ducked back into my own apartment. I hadn't any more than got in there than I heard the elevator stop at the seventh floor. I couldn't understand that, because I knew these people couldn't possibly have had time enough to get up to the seventh floor in the elevator. I waited, listening, and heard you two come down the corridor. I could barely hear the sound of the buzzer in the other apartment. I opened the door to chase you away and saw you were actually entering the apartment, so I had to make a quick excuse, that the sound of the buzzer had wakened me. Then I jerked the door shut. When the four people came up, I really and truly thought you were still in the apartment, and I was dying of curiosity to see what was happening."

"How long had you known him?" Mason asked.

She said sadly, "I loved him. I was the one that he wanted to marry when he left his wife. I don't know how long this other thing had been going on. I became suspicious, and one time when I had an opportunity to go through his pockets, I found a key stamped 'Mandrake Arms Apartment, Number Seven-oh-two.' Then I thought I knew, but I wanted to be sure. I found out who had apartment seven-oh-one and made a proposition for a sublease that simply couldn't be turned down.

"I waited and watched. This brunette walked down the corridor and used *her* key to open the apartment. I slipped out into the corridor and listened at the door. I heard him give her the same old line he'd given me so many times, and my heart turned to bitter acid. I hated him. I killed him . . . and I was caught."

Mason turned to Stewart Linn. "There you are, young man. If you want to be the fearless prosecutor, there's your murderess, but you'll probably never be able to get a jury to think it's anything more than manslaughter."

A much chastened Linn said, "Would you mind telling me how you figured this out, Mr. Mason?"

Mason said, "Clements' key was missing. Obviously he must have had it when he entered the apartment. The murderer must have taken it from his pocket. Why? So he or she could come back. And if what Don Ralston said was true, *someone* must have been in the apartment when he rang the bell from the street, someone who let him in by pressing the buzzer.

"What happened to that someone? I must have been walking down the corridor within a matter of seconds after Ralston had pressed the button on the street door. Yet I saw no one leaving the apartment. There was no one in the corridor. Obviously, then, the person who pressed the buzzer must have had a place to take refuge in another nearby apartment.

"Having reasoned that far, having learned a young, attractive woman had only that very day taken a lease on the apartment opposite, the answer became so obvious it ceased to be a mystery."

Stewart Linn nodded thoughtfully. "Obvious when you have once pointed it out," he said.

Mason picked up his briefcase and smiled at Della Street. "Come on, Della," he said. "Let's get Fay Allison and . . ."

He stopped as he saw Fay Allison's face. "What's happened to *your* lipstick?"

And then his eyes moved over to take in Dane Grover, who was standing by her, his mouth streaked diagonally with a huge red smear.

Fay Allison had neglected to remove the thick coating of lipstick which she had put on when Mason had asked Benjamin Harlan, the identification expert, to take an imprint of her lips. Now the heavy mark where her mouth had been pressed against the mouth of Dane Grover gave an oddly jarring note of incongruity to the entire proceedings.

On the lower floors a mob of eager, curious spectators were baying like hounds on the track of Anita Bonsal. In the courtroom the long, efficient arm of the law was gathering Shirley Tanner into its grasp, and there, amidst the machinery of tragedy, the romance of Fay Allison and Dane Grover picked up where it had left off.

It was the gavel of Judge Randolph Jordan that brought them back to the grim realities of justice, transferred the courtroom from the scene of a dramatic confession to a crowded place, filled with chairs, tables, and benches, peopled by puppets who were mechanically doing the bidding of justice.

"The Court," announced Judge Jordan, "will dismiss the case against Fay Allison. The Court will order Shirley Tanner into custody and the Court will suggest to the Prosecutor that a complaint be issued for Anita Bonsal, upon such charge as may seem expedient to the office of the District Attorney. And the Court does hereby extend its most sincere apologies to the defendant, Fay Allison. And the Court, personally, wishes to congratulate

Mr. Perry Mason upon his brilliant handling of this matter."

There was a moment during which Judge Jordan's stern eyes rested upon the lipstick-smeared countenance of Dane Grover.

A faint smile twitched at the corners of His Honor's mouth.

The gavel banged once more.

"Court," announced Judge Randolph Jordan, "is adjourned."

Fingers of Fong

THERE are very, very few people who have more than the haziest idea of that section of San Francisco which is given over to the residences of the Chinese. There are licensed guides who conduct nightly throngs of tourists to the picturesque segment of the Orient. They assume an air of infinite wisdom and occasionally hint at things they could show if they only dared. But, invariably, they never dare.

They herd their charges through a regular routine tour. While the openmouthed spectator may see the underground passageway which led to the room where, so says the guide, the hatchetmen of the Bing Kungs surprised the defenders of the Hop Sings, the tourist never sees the rooms on either side. While he may be conducted into the outer room of a temple, taken to the shop of a goldsmith, brought to listen to the high, nasal shrill of a sing-song girl, he is never once allowed to leave the beaten path which has been mapped out for him.

Never, by any chance whatever, is he allowed to see Fong Die.

For that matter, the guides do not know of the existence of Fong Die, let alone the place where he is to be found. And to the plainclothes officers, who take care always to be in pairs when they patrol the district, he is little more than a legend.

Dick Sprague was, perhaps, the only white man who

knew Fong Die personally for what he was, who had ever been permitted to call upon the man.

And Dick Sprague, well as he knew his Chinese, never knew exactly why he had been so honored. He knew, of course, that the Chinese do not do things by haphazard guess. They would have had him under close observation for some time before they made the first move; but Dick Sprague had been unaware of such observation.

He knew that he had been employed on one or two rather intricate cases involving matters which pertained to the Chinese. He suspected that certain pitfalls which developed had been shrewdly designed to test his honesty. Then had come the proposition out of a clear sky. He would give up his little private detective agency and work exclusively for the On Leong tong.

At first he had taken it as a joke. But the retainer which was tendered was certainly no joke, and Dick needed the money. He wanted to marry the "sweetest girl in the world," and such a step requires money in a considerable amount.

Bess could never understand the Chinese. Nor could she understand the mystery with which Dick Sprague surrounded his contacts with the race. But she was wise enough to leave matters of business entirely in his hands. Dick, for his part, knew the Chinese well enough to keep his own counsel on all matters pertaining to the business end of his agency.

Which was why he contemplated with some alarm the bit of rice paper which had been slipped into his palm.

They were in a movie theater, sitting in that quiet proximity which characterizes those between whom there is a perfect understanding. The picture was one of those things which dealt with gangsters and machine guns. The sound apparatus was giving off a rapid rattle of machine-gun fire, and neither Bess nor Dick Sprague noticed the shadow that slid stealthily down the aisle, a quiet figure, seeking a seat in the darkened house.

But the figure paused for a fraction of a second in

the aisle, directly opposite Dick Sprague. There was the flash of motion, and the rice paper crumpled into Dick's palm.

Dick gave a convulsive start, turned to survey the aisle, and saw only a shabby figure merging into the darkness of the theater.

He waited until Bess had her attention concentrated on the tense action of the picture, then opened the rice paper. Not that he needed to see what was on it. He knew only too well.

There were a few brush strokes of a camel's-hair brush, the sharp red lines of an engraved seal. Dick knew that the red seal was etched in stone, that it was the private mark of Fong Die, that the camel's-hair brush had formed the complicated characters of the single word *lai,* meaning "come."

That character was a complicated mass of ebony-black strokes, an elongated square on the left side, a daub of miscellaneous lines on the right, divided into upper and lower divisions by lines that came to a point in the center.

Dick Sprague could not read Chinese, but he had seen that fateful character, coupled with the red seal of Fong Die, often enough to know the purport of the command and the necessity for immediate obedience.

He crumpled the rice paper, thrust it into his pocket, and touched Bess on the arm.

"I have to go, dear."

She stared at him, the terror engendered by the stabbing machine guns of the gangster picture showing in her eyes.

"Go where?"

"Business. I've just been summoned."

Her eyes widened.

"It's those Chinese!" she said.

He shrugged his shoulders, stood to one side, and helped her with her coat.

"It's money," he said. "Bread and butter. And we can't quarrel with bread and butter."

She was wordless as he took her from the theater,

and helped her into a cab. She could not argue with the logic of his position, but she resented the authority of that strange power which could summon him so mysteriously and demand such compulsory obedience.

She kept her chin up, her head forward. Her blue eyes were cold and hard. She gave the fur coat a swift jerk, indicating her anger.

"Good night," said Dick.

She gave only an inaudible reply, slammed the door, and then noticed that she had caught the fur coat on the side of the door catch when she had jerked it and had ripped a piece of the smooth fur into a jagged, unsightly tear.

She slumped back on the cushions and gave way to sobs of disappointment and futile rage. It was to have been an undisturbed evening when Dick was to forget business and responsibilities, a night given over to play and laughter. And now she was on her way home in a taxicab.

Dick Sprague walked down dim stairs surrounded with a musty smell of damp earth blended with the peculiar odor which is indescribable, yet which indicates the presence of packed humanity, waiting patiently.

A peanut-oil lamp burned like a flickering star at the end of an underground passage. His guide indicated the lamp with a withered forefinger.

Dick walked to the lamp and paused. He had no fear. If the Chinese had wished to harm him, they had had ample opportunity before. They could have killed him a hundred times over. He realized that these precautions were merely the safeguards with which Fong Die protected himself.

He stood before the peanut-oil lamp, regarding the flickering flame, hearing the retreating footsteps of his guide, his mind in a turmoil, not with the mystery of his surroundings, but with the look that had been on Bessie Delvan's face when she slammed the door of the taxicab.

Yet there was no arguing with a summons of Fong Die.

A section of the wall at his right swung noiselessly to one side.

"Come," said a voice.

Dick entered a sort of underground anteroom in which several people sat motionless upon the hard-seated, straight-backed Chinese chairs which are slow torture to uneducated anatomies. He was ushered up a flight of stairs, through a larger room, along another passage, and a huge door swung quietly open.

The chamber into which Dick entered was filled with furniture that was almost priceless, inlaid with rare mother-of-pearl, carved in intricate designs, capped in carved ivory in which the hands of the artisan had made of the ivory a lacelike border of such delicacy that it seemed as intangible as a bit of white cloud dissolving against the blue of a summer sky.

But the room was entirely dominated by the tall man who sat stiffly erect before a desk-table that would have brought a small fortune at an oriental art auction.

His forehead was smooth and unwrinkled. The beady eyes were filled with that inscrutable patience which reckons things without time. The cheekbones were high, the cheeks hollow, the mouth full and firm.

And the hands seemed more powerful as an index of character than the face. They were long and subtle. Each finger seemed to have a flexible volition of its own. It was as though five serpents had been fastened together and worked in twining unison of purpose.

The lighting was so cleverly done that the room seemed flooded with moonlight, yet no particular source of light could be selected as dominating the illumination. There were many such sources, softened by strings of purest crystal.

The man spoke as Dick came into the room.

"I would not have summoned you from your night of amusement except for the most urgent emergency. That the summons was inopportune will be remembered when the compensation is paid.

"There is a Chinese who is arrested in Santa Barbara. He is charged with murder. His name is Chew Boc Chung. He is clever, and he is a member of the On Leong tong. He has asked for protection and aid, and he shall receive them.

"A man is registered at the Biltmore Hotel under the name of Charles Woo. You will report to him. You will make an immediate investigation. That is all."

The Chinese spoke excellent English in a monotone. During the time that he spoke he never hesitated for a word, nor did he ever look directly at Dick Sprague. He might have been merely a graven statue that could speak. He moved only his hands and his lips. The lips moved to articulate the words; the hands were always restless. They were toying with an ivory and jade ornament, and the fingers seemed to wrap themselves around it as though they were practicing for some more purposeful work. It was as though placid serpents twined themselves about some smooth rock, sunning themselves in amity, twining in smooth grace, yet never letting the beholder forget that they were serpents, and deadly.

Dick Sprague spoke slowly.

"Is the man innocent or guilty?"

"He is innocent."

"Is the evidence damaging to him?"

"It is damning."

"How far shall I go? What is the limit?"

"There is no limit."

Dick Sprague bowed and turned away.

"I am ready," he said.

Instantly, a shadowy figure materialized from the dim corners of the room. A door opened softly, a different door from the one by which Dick had entered. He moved out of the room with its weird lighting, similar to moonlight, its magnificent furniture, and the strange figure that spoke in a monotone and seemed like some colossal mind, without feeling or emotion, a thinking mechanism of unblemished perfection, housed in a tall, slender body which remained motionless, save for the fingers.

Dick Sprague emerged upon a side street which sloped down the steep hill toward the bay. The lights of boats were visible far out on the water. The dark sidewalks ran into the lighted cross streets where gaping tourists stared at the things which had been prepared for them to stare at.

An automobile was waiting, the motor running.

Dick Sprague stepped into the back of the closed car. The multi-cylindered power of the machine rippled into motion. The car glided down the steep slope of the street, lurched sharply to the right, and threaded its way through the traffic of the lighted street.

The car turned again. The speed constantly increased. The driver was wonderfully skillful. Dick Sprague, leaning back against the cushions, was thinking of Bessie Delvan. He knew that he was being piloted to the airport, and he wondered if he would have a chance to telephone Bess, and, if he did have a chance, what he could say that would help matters any.

But he had no chance to telephone. The car went through gates that were held open by a man in uniform. It swung out to a lighted circle of cement where a cabin plane was glowing like a huge silver beetle. The prop was a blur of motion.

The car slid to the side of the cabin door. The driver opened the door of the car. Dick stepped into the cabin of the plane, and the door slammed. He was conscious of a dark figure silhouetted against the illumination from the front of the plane. He knew that this figure was moving the controls.

The plane roared into jolting motion, inclined sharply, slanted upward, and banked. The lights of San Francisco showed as an urn of molten metal. Then, across the bay, Oakland, Alameda, and Berkeley were as seas of fused constellations. Between lay the black mystery of the bay.

Dick Sprague sighed, adjusted his body to the cushioned seat, and tried to get some sleep. He had gone on these expeditions before, and he knew that the pilot would be extremely skillful, that the plane would be of the fastest type, that the pilot would not talk, and that, until the case was concluded, there would be little rest for the detective who was employed by the On Leong tong in the protection of its members.

Dick dozed off. He awoke once or twice to look down on a black landscape, broken here and there by little splotches of light which indicated cities, by revolving beacons whose changes of color flash represented definite signals of location. The pilot knew where they were. Dick did not. There was nothing to tell whether the ground below was plain or mountain. It was merely a black mystery, stretching under a star-studded sky.

It was after midnight when Sprague presented himself at the office of the sheriff of Santa Barbara County. The deputy in charge was kindly but grim.

"Looks like a perfect case against him," he said.

Dick Sprague puffed on a cigar. The deputy puffed on its mate. The cigar was as good as money could buy. The night was calm, and there were no calls coming in to the sheriff's office.

"Tell me about it," said Dick. "As much, that is, as you can tell."

The deputy mouthed the cigar, and turned to Dick.

"Your man was a collector from Los Angeles. He had an appointment with the murdered woman, Mrs. Pelman-Swift. The appointment shows on the appointment book, and your man doesn't deny it. The appointment was for seven-thirty. He kept it on the dot. She'd taken out some of her most valuable treasures. She wanted to sell the lot.

"Chew Boc Chung went into the private sitting room which adjoined her bedroom. Nobody knows what happened. There were voices. The servant can't remember hearing the woman speak in particular but remembers hearing the Chinese talking, as though he was driving a bargain.

"Then Chew Boc Chung left. He left his check for three hundred and fifty dollars on the table. As he went out he told the servant that her mistress didn't want to be disturbed for an hour.

"The servant was suspicious of something in his manner. The request was unusual. She decided to take a peek in the room and see why her mistress should be so particular against intrusion. She noticed Mrs. Pelman-Swift sitting in a peculiarly rigid position on the couch, her head down, apparently sleeping.

"So she waited for half an hour and looked in again. The position was unchanged. She went in, alarmed by the position, and found the woman was dead, strangled by a fine silken cord that had been looped around the neck and drawn tight.

"There was a little screen placed in front of the couch, as though to screen the corpse from anyone who might be sitting in the room. The collection of Chinese jades and carvings had been in a steel lockbox. The cover of the box was open. Mrs. Pelman-Swift had opened it herself. Apparently that had been about the last thing she'd done on earth. Most of the really valuable pieces of the collection were missing.

"We found the man we wanted. He had registered at the Biltmore—high-class Chinese he is, too. He wouldn't make any statement.

"We searched his room and didn't find any of the missing stuff. But somebody got the bright idea that he might have mailed it. So we got the post-office authorities to cooperate. They found that several packages had been mailed from a box near the house where the woman had been murdered.

"These packages were sent as first-class mail. Three of them were to Chew Boc Chung. See what he'd done? He'd simply mailed the stuff to himself. Pretty clever. We opened the packages addressed to him and found part of the loot. It wasn't the most valuable part. He seems to have concealed that in some other way. Those Chinks are clever.

"But the stuff we've got will hang him all right. We've got a perfect case. The medical examiner places the time of death at just about the time the servant can testify that Chew Boc Chung walked into the room.

"We've got a theory that one of the pieces she had was of some sacred significance. It was a museum piece from the Forbidden City. She'd been asked to sell it and wouldn't do it. Chew Boc Chung knew he had to have that piece. Probabilities are he'd been sent to get it. He knew she wouldn't sell, and he didn't waste any time. Anyhow, that piece has gone. It's carved jade, very valuable as jade, but it's got some sacred significance."

Dick Sprague chose his words cautiously. "Rather far-fetched. He could have bought the stuff he mailed to himself."

The deputy grinned. "Wait until you see what a local jury has to say about that!"

Sprague pressed the point. "He must have left that three-hundred-and-fifty-dollar check there for something."

"Uh huh," said the deputy, and grinned. "It shows that she was alive when he gave it to her, and she wasn't when he left. That's all you need to worry about in putting up a case before a jury here."

"How about the servant?"

"Nope. The servant's an old woman, one of those hatchet-faced relics that get in a family and stay there. She's been with Mrs. Pelman-Swift for twenty years. The mistress was no spring chicken, you know. She was one of those women who have ice blood and efficiency in their veins. Managed her own business, kept appointment books, and all that.

"But mainly the servant's out of the question because she didn't have the physical strength. It was a man's job. Grabbing the woman and putting that silk cord about her neck was something that took agility and strength."

Dick Sprague tried another tack. "Did you get any fingerprints?"

"Now, son, you're askin' for something that I can't talk about. I can give you the facts the way the newspaper boys are gettin' 'em, but I can't let you in on the inside of any dope the district attorney may be keeping on ice."

Dick nodded.

"You got the jewel box here?" he asked.

"Yes"—the deputy grinned—"and it's out of sight. If you saw that, you'd see the latents on it and know all about the fingerprint dope."

Dick Sprague acknowledged the correctness of the statement with an unenthusiastic nod.

"Anything else you've got that the newspaper boys are getting to see?"

"Got the appointment book."

"What does it show?"

"That this Chinese art dealer had an appointment for seven-thirty."

"Let's see it," said Sprague, conscious of the fact that it would be several hours before he could continue his investigation, save in such quarters as were open during the twenty-four-hour period.

The deputy opened a locked strongbox and took out a leather book marked "Appointments." It was held in two segments by an elastic band. When the book was opened at the line of these two segments, the appointments which the murdered woman had had on the day of her death appeared.

The deputy indicated the fateful name of Chew Boc Chung with the end of a pencil.

"There you are. See, she's got Chew Boc Chung's name written there, and then under the memo she's got 'purchase of Chinese art goods.' "

Dick Sprague scowled.

"She had plenty of money. Why did she want to sell her art stuff?"

The deputy snickered.

"She was just like all the rest of 'em. She got in over her necktie in the stock market. She had a tip on something or other—I've forgotten just which it was now—and she sunk all her ready cash in it. The market took a bad turn and wiped her out. She had lots of stuff left, in trust. She could get the income. That's all.

"She needed some ready cash, and it looked like a good time to dispose of some of the Chinese stuff. That's the story I get from the old housekeeper.

"Here . . . see this name on the appointment book? Franklin Welm, appointment at nine o'clock? Well, that's the lad who was handling her stock for her. She was to see him tonight. He came rushing up from Los Angeles to keep the appointment.

"She had given him nearly half a million to invest in stock. He advised her against it, said he was dead certain that stock was unsound and was going to be smashed flat as a pancake. She insisted and made him do it for her. He bought the stock. It was just like he said. The bottom caved right out from under.

"That was two days ago. Looks as though somebody who wanted to unload had given her a buying tip and then shoveled it onto her."

Dick Sprague was staring at the appointment book where the finely written, angular scrawl of the aged woman appeared in delicate tracery.

"Why," he asked, "would she write down a nine o'clock appointment and then write down a seven-thirty appointment after it? The logical way would have been to have written down the earlier appointment first, and then the later one."

The deputy yawned.

"Yeah," he said. "I guess so, but it ain't nothing to us. What we want is to show the whole chain of evidence, that this Chinese curio dealer had the appointment for the time he went there. Shows premeditation and all that. And it shows that she'd have the art stuff out for him."

But Dick Sprague was bending over the page, examining it with squinted eyes.

"Got a little magnifying glass around here?" he asked.

"Yeah, I guess so. Whatcha see, fingerprint or something?"

Dick took the magnifying glass the deputy handed him from the drawer, wiped off the dusty lens, and held it over the appointment book.

"Take a look at this," he said.

The deputy peered forward, the half-smoked cigar held between first and second fingers.

"Huh?" he asked.

"This has been changed. See. It was originally a seven o'clock appointment. Now it's a nine o'clock. But it was changed from a seven into a nine. That's why it appears before the seven-thirty appointment with the Chinese."

The deputy scratched his nose with the hand that held the cigar, got a wisp of smoke in his eye, rubbed it vigorously, then looked again.

"Well," he said dubiously, "there may be something to it. Looks like that loop on the nine had been made with two strokes all right. I ain't no handwriting expert, but that's the way she looks to me. Not that it makes a darn bit of difference. She might have made the appointment for then and changed her mind. Or she might have made the appointment and then found out that it didn't suit Welm. Anyhow, Welm ain't mixed up in it. He said his appointment was for nine o'clock, and he showed up here at nine. He drove up from Los Angeles."

Dick Sprague produced another cigar from his inside pocket and handed it to the deputy.

"Now this Franklin Welm," he asked, "did he go back to Los Angeles?"

"Nope. He went down to a hotel here in town. Left an address. Said we could get him there if he could do anything. He seemed to be all smashed up over the murder. Said he didn't like the old lady particularly, that she was obstinate and greedy, but that she was a good customer.

That she'd dropped a bunch of cash on the last flier, but that she had more money coming in under the trust fund in about three or four months, and that he knew she'd make a gamble with that and that he'd get the business."

Dick's fingers were drumming idly on the battered desk. He looked over at the angular writing on the appointment book.

"Suppose," he said, "you should get him over here and we should just take the precaution of checking up on where he was at the actual time of the murder."

The deputy pursed his lips.

"Well," he said, "I wouldn't want to take the responsibility myself. But I guess I could get it done okay. In fact, the sheriff's been to Los Angeles on some business. He's going to look in at the office here when he comes up. He's due almost any minute. Stick around and you can talk to him."

The suite in the Biltmore was thick with the smell of joss sticks. Incense burners eddied lazy smoke curls up into the atmosphere.

Charles Woo sat on an overstuffed chair in unblinking attentiveness. Fong Die, tall, erect in the plain, straight-backed chair, toyed with a pencil, and his long, caressing fingers seemed to envelope the pencil, twist it, turn it with a motion that was almost a menace.

There was a subtle threat about those long, twining fingers.

Dick Sprague, eyes red from lack of sleep, feet planted apart on the floor, jaw thrust grimly forward, made his report.

"That's the reason I sent for you to come down here. I'm satisfied this man Welm did the job, but I'm afraid I can't prove it. That's partially true because the county authorities think they've got an ironclad case against Chew Boc Chung, and they don't want to do anything that'll get him out of it."

Charles Woo glanced at the sage of the On Leong tong, then back at Dick Sprague.

"The alibi?" he asked softly.

"Faked. It looks good, but it isn't airtight, not by a long ways. Welm had an appointment for seven o'clock. He came up here, kept that appointment, and killed the woman. Then he changed the hour of the appointment in the book, took some of the Chinese art things, put them in parcels and addressed 'em to Chew Boc Chung in Los Angeles, and stuck 'em in the mailbox.

"He figured that the Chinese wouldn't make a report when he found the woman dead, not when he realized what he was up against, and that the death had been done by strangling with a silk cord. He figured the Chinese would get out of the picture and keep out of sight."

Charley Woo sighed.

Fong Die wrapped his fingers about the pencil a trifle more rapidly.

"That is true," he said softly, "more true than you know. For this woman did have an article of Chinese art that had been taken from the Forbidden City. The honor of the Chinese demanded that it be returned. She had refused offers for it before. Chew Boc Chung had determined to regain that article of art. It was the will of the On Leongs."

Dick Sprague jerked his head in an emphatic gesture of affirmation.

"Of course," he rasped, "I figure that this Welm is a smooth bird. He's pretty much on the inside. What I think he did is to bucket-shop that stock order. See what happened? She gave him quarter of a million to buy a stock that he knew was going down. He tried to get her not to do it. She insisted. He just pocketed the money, reported to her that he'd bought the stock, then held off delivery for a couple of days until this stock went down in a crash.

"Then he told her that she'd lost the stock money, and, seeing the ticker reports, she knew it was true. But she was just cagey enough to check up on him, and she was pretty close to the truth. So she got him up here for a showdown.

"He stood to lose a quarter of a million as well as be convicted of embezzlement. So he simplified matters by removing her, framing the crime so it would look as though Chew Boc Chung did it. He had a plane cached out here somewhere. He took it back to Los Angeles or Hollywood, climbed in a car, and made speed up here. He can show where he bought gas in Ventura at twenty minutes past eight, where he bought five gallons before that at the foot of the Conejo grade.

"That makes a good alibi, but it's suspicious in itself. A man wouldn't have bought two five-gallon orders of gasoline so close together. He hasn't any explanation to offer for that. Says he just bought five gallons at the Conejo grade station and then thought he'd better have more.

"He didn't go all the way back in his plane, just far enough to give him an alibi. Come to think of it, he's probably got a secret landing field somewhere over the Conejo country.

"Anyhow, that's the only theory I can work out that gives Chew Boc Chang a chance."

Dick stared over at Charley Woo.

"Was she alive when Chew Boc Chang went into the room?" asked Fong Die.

Charley Woo shook his head.

"She was dead. But Chew Boc Chang knew that the crime would be framed on him and that some of the art treasures would probably be found in his baggage. He sensed that these would only be minor pieces. Therefore, he tried to leave a check for three hundred and fifty dollars so that it would appear he had purchased these articles.

"He was afraid to raise an alarm because he thought she was asleep when he first entered the room, and he wanted to take advantage of her slumber to look into the collection. The box was open, and he pulled it over to him and looked at it. Afterward he realized that his fingerprints were on the box."

Charley Woo spoke in smooth, polished English, the English of one who speaks several languages.

The long fingers of Fong Die twisted themselves about the pencil.

"He is clever, this Welm, but he is a criminal, and the crime is one of greed. More than that, he is one who murders to conceal crime.

"There is a saying among the Chinese that hunger is satisfied by food, while greed is only inflamed by gain."

He stopped speaking, and his voice was as solemn as that of a priest. It seemed that the room with its smell of incense and joss sticks reverberated with the sound of that voice for several seconds after it had ceased to make intelligible words.

Dick Sprague looked at the sage of the On Leongs and saw nothing upon his face. The features were absolutely bland and expressionless.

Charles Woo nodded his head slowly.

"The man is greedy. He could not bear to pass up the talisman of jade. But he is also cunning, too cunning for these white officers. They will do nothing to help us. Unofficially we can do nothing. The situation calls for strategy."

Fong Die spoke slowly.

"It has been written that the knowledge of guilt is akin to panic, and that panic robs the brain of cunning. It is necessary, therefore, to rob the brain of this man of its cunning. Then we can act."

He reached one of his hands into the sleeve of his jacket, fumbled a short while, then took out a green object and laid it on the table. Dick Sprague moved forward to examine it.

He saw a circle of carved jade, a circle that was bounded with gold filigree. The carving was most cleverly done. It depicted two dragons, apparently struggling in combat. Between the two was a spherical object with little streamers radiating from it.

Fong Die regarded him speculatively.

"Here," he said, "is the duplicate of the piece of carved jade which the dead woman possessed. It had been stolen from the Forbidden City. This piece is the mate. It shows the two dragons engaged in struggle for the fiery pearl. On the other piece of jade the position of the dragons is reversed. The two, taken together, are of sacred significance. This piece is priceless. So is the other."

Dick Sprague leaned forward eagerly.

"Listen," he said, "if I should put on an aviator's costume and get into Welm's room here in the hotel, and let him catch me making a search . . . and he should find this on me! See, he wouldn't know it was a duplicate. He's hidden the real piece somewhere. If he finds it on me, and sees the aviator's helmet and leather coat, he'll think that I've checked up on him. He'll betray himself. Then we can get a confession."

Fong Die's long, tapering fingers pushed the carved jade toward Dick Sprague.

"It is priceless," he said, "and the On Leongs trust you with it."

Then his long fingers reached for the teapot, and Dick Sprague knew that the interview was over. But as Sprague was taking his ceremonious farewell, his two hands clasped in front of him, Chinese fashion, the long fingers of Fong Die, which had been toying off and on with the pencil, tightened, as twining snakes might tighten about the body of a rabbit.

As Sprague stepped into the hall, he heard the snapping click of broken wood. The long fingers had broken the pencil.

Dick Sprague sat in the room at the hotel. About him was a litter of wreckage. The mattress had been ripped apart. Baggage had been opened and the contents strewn about the floor. Drawers had been pulled from dresser and bureau.

It was in that hour when dusk commences to give way to darkness, and the mystery of the semitropic night was seeping into the dark corners of the room.

In the ceiling was a dictograph, with wires leading to an adjoining room where two deputies sat in bored inactivity.

Dick Sprague had been able to get that much from the sheriff's office. But he could get no more. The web of circumstantial evidence had closed about Chew Boc Chung, and the authorities regarded the case as closed.

There were steps outside.

Dick Sprague crouched on the floor, his hand exploring the mattress.

A key clicked. The door was flung open and the figure of a man on the threshold was outlined in sharp silhouette against the lighted corridor. There was a startled gasp, then the light switch snapped. The room was flooded with brilliance and Dick Sprague found himself staring into the business end of an automatic.

"Burglar, eh?" said Franklin Welm.

Dick Sprague got to his feet and blinked. His face showed chagrin.

"Call it that, if you want to," he said doggedly.

Welm sneered, staring about him at the wreckage of the room.

"Find anything worth taking?" he asked, and closed the door behind him.

Dick Sprague shrugged his shoulders.

Welm studied the aviator's helmet, the leather coat.

"Been flying, eh?"

"Some."

"Far?"

"Just investigating the places around the Conejo grade where a man could have sat a crate down and picked up a car. That's all."

Welm grunted and approached Sprague.

"Get 'em up in the air," he said, "and get 'em up high!"

Dick reached for the ceiling.

Welm came to him, thrust the gun into his stomach, then started to explore the pockets of Sprague's clothes. He took a gun and tossed it on the wrecked bed. His questing hands discovered the credentials which identified Dick Sprague as a detective. He read them, sneered, and tossed them, too, on the bed. Then he encountered the carved jade talisman.

He stared at it, his face twisting with emotion.

"Where did you get that?" he asked.

"Where you'd concealed it," said Sprague. "I've punctured your alibi, Welm. You changed the time of the appointment in the appointment book. You committed the murder and then built an alibi. But your greed betrayed you. You held out the most valuable of the art curios."

Franklin Welm stepped back. The automatic was in his right hand. The left held the carved jade talisman. His face was white. His forehead glistened with perspiration.

"You lie," he said.

Dick shrugged his shoulders. "Well," he observed, "we'll just go to jail and talk it over with the authorities, see what they have to say."

Welm's mouth twitched. His eyes showed panic, then sudden blind decision.

"Like hell we will," he said. "I thought I'd covered my tracks. But I'd left open a channel of escape if I hadn't. You'll never testify against me, and this damned jade won't ever come into evidence against me!"

Dick knew the chances he had taken when he entered that room. The great danger was, of course, that the man would resort to violence before assistance could arrive. He knew now that the man before him intended to pull the trigger on that automatic.

"Quick!" he shouted, and flung himself to one side.

The gun roared, the bullet almost creasing Dick's check. Then the door of the adjoining room crashed open.

"In the name of the law . . ."

The voice did not finish. Welm had whirled and fired. There was the sound of a bullet impacting flesh. The man staggered back, crashed to the floor. Another gun boomed. There was the sound of running feet, then more shots. A police whistle shrilled. From the street came the sound of a motor grinding into swift speed.

Dick ran to the door of the room.

One of the deputies was sprawled out on the floor, breathing in gasps, writhing and twisting. The other was coming back up the stairs, his face white.

"Got away!" he said. "Good heavens, who'd have thought he'd pull a stunt like that! Smoked his way out. Poor Bob . . . looks bad . . . hope he'll pull through. Get the ambulance. I'll notify the office and have the highways closed. We'll get that dirty murderer."

Dick Sprague had retrieved his gun from the bed. He ran to the lobby of the hotel which was in an uproar. The siren of an ambulance sounded from the street outside.

Dick followed the ambulance to the hospital. He saw nothing of two Chinese tongmen who had been stationed in front of the hotel. After he found that the deputy would probably recover, he walked to the sheriff's office and listened to the telephoned reports from various officers who had closed the main highways from the city. Those reports were merely routine. There was no sign of Franklin Welm.

It was not until three o'clock in the morning that the police located him. He was found then near a plane in a secret landing field which had been located off the north of the Conejo grade.

He was quite dead.

The sheriff received the telephone report from the searching parties who had located the field and the body. They had seen a flare, heard the noise of a motor, and had investigated. In the darkness, after the flare, it had taken some time to find the place. Then they had discovered the plane and the body.

"How'd he die?" asked the sheriff.

The receiver rattled forth an answer.

"I'll be out," said the officer. "Wait there. Don't let anyone touch anything. Okay. G'bye."

He hung up the receiver and reached for his hat.

Dick Sprague ventured a few questions.

"What killed him?" he asked.

"Choked," said the sheriff. "There were finger marks on his throat."

Dick Sprague thought of the crushed pencil.

"Any peculiarities about them?" he asked. "The finger marks, I mean. I wondered if they were . . . oh, maybe very long fingers."

The sheriff shook his head.

"You can't tell, I don't s'pose. Just finger marks. They'd be long bruise marks, just showing how he died."

"I see," said Sprague.

"Gang killing probably," the sheriff said, and went out.

It was in San Francisco that Bessie Delvan showed him the new fur coat. "It came by messenger. There wasn't any card in it at all. It was a young Chinese boy. He just said it was for me, to take the place of the one I'd torn when I got in the cab. But I don't know how they could have known that."

Dick Sprague stared at the gloss of the expensive coat.

"Anybody with the messenger?" he asked.

"Yes," she said, "a Chinese, rather tall and slender, with the most remarkable hands I've ever seen on a man. He had two funny rings, one on each hand. They were jade spheres with gold all around the edges, and they were carved with dragons. The dragons seemed to be struggling for a sort of pearl that was embedded in the center. . . . Did you have a successful trip?"

Dick answered the question with another question.

"You're sure there were two jade rings?"

"Yes. They were huge. There was one on each hand."

Dick sighed.

"I guess my trip was okay. I exposed a cunning murderer and prevented an innocent Chinese from being hanged."

The girl nodded. Her eyes were dreamy.

"Funny," she said slowly, "about those fingers. They seemed alive, somehow, like snakes."

Dick Sprague thought of the dark marks on the throat of the murderer, of the two jade ornaments which graced the long fingers.

"Perhaps," he said, "they were fingers of fate."

But he did not explain his remark, nor did he tell the girl she had been one of the few whites to see Fong Die, the sage of the On Leongs, the man who was filled with mercy for the innocent, a veritable fiend incarnate for the guilty.

"It's a fine coat," he said.

The Valley of Little Fears

THIS thing is true of the desert: the first time you feel its spell you'll either love it or you'll hate it. If you hate it, your hatred will be founded on fear.

Those who know the desert claim you never change that original reaction, no matter how long you live in the sandy wastes. In that they're wrong. I know of one case where the rule didn't work. The desert is hard to figure, and you can't make rules about it.

I know the story of the man who wore a dog collar around his neck and who lived in the valley of little fears. And the story is known to but few people.

Not that they didn't know of the dog collar. He wore his shirt buttoned at the neck, trying to hide what was underneath. But he forgot himself once or twice and men got a glimpse of the leather collar, studded with little rivets of polished metal, with the silver nameplate on the back.

After that the news traveled as it does in the desert, little whispers seeping from place to place with incredible speed. The desert's like that, a place of whispers. The sand drifts along on the dry desert winds and rustles against the stalks of the cactus. It sounds as though someone was whispering. Then, when the wind gets stronger, the sand rustles across the sand with the strangest whisper of all: sand talking to sand.

I've lain in my blankets many a night and listened to the sand whispers. Sometimes you think you can catch a word here and there. Perhaps, just before you're dropping off to sleep, you'll hear a whole sentence. It'll pop into your mind just like someone breathed it in your ear. But no one's there. It's just the sand whispering to the sand.

It happened up near the Armagosa Sink, which is over east of Death Valley. Between the Funeral Mountains and the Kingston Range, nature went crazy. The Armagosa Creek is a freak in itself. And there's miles of cinders, and a place they call Ash Meadows because it's a great stretch of volcanic ash. Then there are weird mountains colored with reds and browns and mineral greens. There's no vegetation to speak of.

Most of the springs are poisonous. The country is filled with all sorts of metal. There are a few mines that employ help, a few individual prospects that keep some old desert rats busy. And these men have their little gathering places. They have a saloon that is a saloon, not an imitation. They have a dance hall where women come, stay for a while, and then go. Even the dance-hall girls can't stand the country very long.

And over all is silence and sunlight.

Human nature gets worn to the raw, and civilization is forgotten. The barren hills twist weird forms of volcanic spires into the hot sky. The little desert winds, hissing down the slopes of the mountains, bite deep into the sand and send it whispering and scampering over the plain. The desert rules.

It was into this place that Fred Smith came.

He gave his name as Fred Smith, and his eyes remained downcast as he spoke the words. We knew that this was not his name, knew also that he was alien to the game of inventing false names.

In his eyes there was a great fear, a nameless dread that cropped out once in a while and was then stifled back into the dark depths of his soul. He feared the desert, and he feared something that he had left behind. It was stark fear that had driven him into the waste spaces, and it was fear that held him here.

They gave him a job at the Red Bonanza Mine. It was a job on the surface. Such men don't do good work in the dark solitude of an underground drift.

One morning Nick Cryder rambled up to the mine to look him over. Nick was the deputy sheriff who had charge of the district and he was plenty hard-boiled, as a man had to be with his job. I happened to be present when Nick dropped in.

"Newcomer, eh?" said Cryder.

Smith was making some entries in the time book. His hand started to shake so much that the pen wobbled off the line.

"Yes, sir," he answered, his eyes fastened on the silver star that Nick had pinned to his vest.

"Where you from?"

"Los Angeles."

"What'd you leave there for?"

"Just to get away from—lots of things—nothing wrong. Just because I wasn't having the chance I needed to build up my character. I wanted to come out into the open places and begin all over again."

Nick fastened him with eyes that were cold and hard in their disbelief.

"I'll check up on you. If you're on the dodge I'll get the goods on you." And he strode out.

I waited until Smith raised his eyes. "I wouldn't let men talk to you like that, Smith. The boys around here will get you tabbed as a coward if you let Nick Cryder ride you around the reservation with his spurs on."

"What could I do?" he said. "The man's an officer."

"Cryder's a bully," I told him. "Nearly all men are bullies. You get just the sort of treatment you expect in this world. You act like a cur that expects to be kicked and you'll get kicked. And in this country men kick harder and faster than any other place in the world."

I thought that might buck him up. It didn't.

Smith kept on assisting the timekeeper. Cryder saw him twice and took occasion to ride him both times. Men lisened and sneered. After that they all rode Smith—and made him like it.

He had a little cabin up a valley back of the mine. It had been an old prospector's place. The prospector and the mine owners had tangled in court, and one night the prospector was shot. Cryder had never done much about the shooting. Cryder was crooked, of course. A deputy sheriff who hangs around a camp where gambling and saloons run wide open has to be crooked, or just dumb. Cryder wasn't dumb.

I dropped in to see Smith one Sunday afternoon; I thought I'd cheer him up a bit. It was no use. He sat there in the dark cabin, the stuffy air smelling of human occupancy and stale cooking, with his head in his hands. A dog crouched at his feet. It was a police dog, after a fashion, but its spirit had been broken.

When I stepped on the board porch in front of the cabin Smith jumped to his feet, his face stark with fear. The dog tucked his tail between his legs and crawled under the table. I could see the yellow gleam of its eyes.

"Got a dog, eh?"

"Oh, it's you! Yes. I found him a couple of days ago. He was running down the street, with some kids throwing rocks at him. I sympathized with him and brought him home."

I thought of the little town sprawled out in the blistering sun, the dusty street, the temper of the urchins who had learned to curse almost as soon as they had learned to talk.

"A dog of his size that would stand his ground wouldn't have rocks thrown at him," I said.

He nodded, but the nod didn't have any interest. I talked with him awhile and left. I spat in the dust and washed my hands of both of them.

It was Big Bertha who made the next move in the game. Big Bertha didn't fit into the picture the way you'd have expected. She drifted into the city, opened a lunch counter, and bucked the competition of the restaurants, putting them out of business, and making the other one change cooks.

Cryder tried to throw a scare into Big Bertha. She heard what he had to say, then she spoke her piece:

"Listen, you tin-star braggart! I come here to mind my own business. I'm on the square. I quit a circus, where I handled everything from elephants to lions, and I ain't going to let no four-flusher bluff me out now. If you don't like my competition—buy me out! If the bootleg twins who tried to corner the trade in the restaurant business want to get rough, I'll get rough too!"

Cryder had called on her in an effort to stick her for some fancy license under a city ordinance he'd thought up. The city wasn't incorporated. Big Bertha had refused to pay.

I was in Bertha's place when she saw the dog. It was the first time Smith had brought him into town.

"No dogs," said Bertha when Smith came to the door.

He nodded and turned into the little screened porch that kept out the flies. The dog lay down just back of him.

"Ham-and," he said.

She broke the eggs and put them on the fire.

There was a yelp. They both looked up, Big Bertha and Fred Smith. The dog was running down the street with his tail between his legs. Harry Fane was standing by the door, banging rocks at him and laughing.

"That's Fred Smith's dog," said Big Bertha.

Fane came in and slid onto a stool.

"I don't give a damn whose dog he is. When I want to

bang a rock at a dog, I do it. You got anything to say, Smith?"

Smith kept his eyes down on the counter.

After a while Big Bertha turned back to the stove. Fred's ham-and was done. She slid it over to him. Smith ate in a hurry. He wanted to get out. Bertha looked at me and shrugged her big shoulders.

The dog came back whining, looking for Smith, afraid to go near the place, circling around out of stone's throw. Big Bertha dried her hands on her apron and went to the door.

"Come here," she said.

The dog paused, watching her with yellow eyes. She picked up a scrap of meat and whistled. He came then, crawling the last of the distance on his belly, making little whining noises with his mouth. Bertha gave him the meat and watched him.

Fane got to the floor and stamped his foot. The dog yelped and turned to run. Fane laughed. Big Bertha turned to him.

"When I'm making friends with a dog," she said, cold and level like, "you keep yourself outa my affairs. That's a good dog. He's been ruined somewhere and made to be afraid of everybody and everything."

Fane met her eyes, hesitated. He had things pretty much the way he wanted them in this little desert town. Fane controlled the liquor and the dance halls. He stood in with Cryder, of course.

"Don't go gettin' hard," he mumbled.

Big Bertha snorted. Then she called the dog back.

"It ain't right for a dog to associate with a man that's afraid," she told Smith.

"Who says I'm afraid?" asked Smith, finishing up his ham and eggs in a big gulp.

"I do," said Big Bertha.

Smith pushed a coin over the counter and hurried out.

Big Bertha held the dog's collar. "You stay here with me," she told it.

I tried to interfere. "That dog's the only companion Fred Smith's got."

"I can't help it," she said. "I like animals. This dog has got too much in him to be ruined just so some man won't be lonesome. He was a good dog once. Probably got lost or was stolen by somebody who didn't understand dogs. He lost his self-respect. The man probably beat him when he should only have talked with him. The dog got some little fear, and then he got another little fear, and finally it got to be a big fear, and then fear got to be a habit."

"You can't cure him now," I warned her, interested in spite of myself. "Take Fane, for instance—that dog'll always be afraid of Fane, as long as he lives."

Fane laughed. He was the sort of fellow who got a kick out of having people and dogs afraid of him.

Big Bertha snorted at us both. "Shows all you know about it! Of course I couldn't make him overcome a big fear just by reasoning with him or struggling with him. But I can find out the little fears and get him to conquering them. After that the big ones will take care of themselves. Fear and doubt are just habits an animal picks up."

Big Bertha led the dog back of the counter and began talking to it. Her voice was low but packed with authority. The dog whined at her as though he was trying to answer. They were talking to each other when I went out the door.

Twice in the next week I saw the dog. Both times he was running. I didn't actually see Fane throw anything the first time. The second time I saw the motion of his arm as he flung a stone. He was laughing when he went into Bertha's place. I followed him in.

"Fane," I said, "you lay off that dog."

He looked at me with eyes that were menacing in their hostility.

"Your business?" he asked.

"I'm making it my business."

"Maybe," said Fane, "he's a brother of yours."

He dodged my left. His right hand was clawing at a shoulder holster under his armpit. My right connected. He staggered back, skidded over a stool, crashed into the wall, and hit the floor. As he went down his right hand came free, and I caught the glitter of blued steel.

I was unarmed. Folks don't carry hardware with 'em in the desert any more, not as a rule. There was just a chance I could fling one of the stools and block the bullet. I grabbed the nearest stool.

"That'll be all for this time," remarked Big Bertha casually, leaning over the counter. She had a sawed-off shotgun in her hands, and the twin muzzles were pointing right at Fane's stomach. He lowered the gun.

Cryder came on the run. He sided with Fane; that was to be expected. They fined me fifty dollars and gave me a suspended sentence of thirty days—disturbing the peace, assault and battery. They tried to hang a felony charge of assault with a deadly weapon on Big Bertha, but she outfoxed them. She packed up and said she was going down to see the grand jury. Cryder almost got down on his knees to her.

I told Bertha I was sorry, but I always hated to see a man pick on a dog. She shrugged her big shoulders.

"That's for the dog to settle," she told me, speaking casually as though she was talking about a growing child's education. "If a dog expects he's going to be kicked, there'll always be somebody to kick him. A man's got to respect himself to get respect from others. It's the same way with a dog."

He was lying on the floor at her feet. It seemed as though he understood every word she said.

I commented on it.

"Sure he understands," said Big Bertha. "He's a smart dog. That's one of the troubles with him: he's too sensitive. But he's going to work out of it all right."

The dog whined eagerly.

"Named him yet?" I asked.

" 'Growls,' " she answered.

"A heck of a name. Should have called him 'Yelps.' "

She frowned. "That's intended as a wisecrack, I guess, but it ain't funny."

It was three weeks before I saw Fane and the dog together again. Fred Smith was with me. He was servile in his desire to square himself. He talked too much and too fast. I listened to about half of it—some long-winded explanation about his nerves and his health.

He saw the dog in front of Bertha's place and whistled. The dog came trotting across the street. He was glad to see Fred, no mistake about that.

Halfway across the street a rock skidded the dust just under his belly. I looked at the corner. Fane was picking up another rock.

Fred Smith got white in the face. He looked from me to Fane, from Fane to the dog.

I remembered what Bertha had said about its being up to the dog; but I remembered some other things about Fane, and I started for the corner. They could unsuspend that jail sentence. Fane and I were due for an argument, and this time there was something under my own left armpit. This argument was going just as far as Fane wanted it to go.

But the dog was the one that settled things.

He acted for a second as though he wanted to run. Then he turned, hesitated, growled, and the growl reassured him. He started for Fane, and Fane's hand dropped the rock as though it had been hot. When the dog saw Fane was afraid, he charged.

Fane's right hand went for his holster. The dog crouched, with a yellow gleam of hatred in his eyes. Fane glanced over his shoulder, saw a saloon door swing invitingly, and popped in. The dog sprang just as the door closed.

I looked at Fred Smith. The expression on his face was

a mixture of pride and shame—pride for the dog, shame for himself.

I walked over and told Big Bertha about it. Smith went with me.

Bertha was calm. "He's been getting over his little fears," she said. "Now he's ready to tackle some big ones. He'll get cured fast now. It ain't so much of a trick to train animals if you just have patience and realize that habit is the most powerful thing in the world."

Fred Smith leaned over the counter. He spoke so fast the words all ran together:

"Could you do it with me? Could you take me and cure me of whatever is the matter with me? I'd be just like a dog. I'd put myself in your charge, do everything you said. I'd give anything if I could only be like other men and have respect. It's been hell . . ."

Big Bertha stared at him.

"You'd have to have something to make you remember you were being trained," she told him, "something that was with you all the time—a glove on your right hand or something like that."

"I'd do anything," said Fred.

"I wonder if you would?" she mused, and her eyes were narrowed in thought.

I got out. It seemed as though they were better off alone. I began to wonder if Bertha's mother instinct wasn't making her take too much interest in this apology of a man, who had been ruined by fear and had now come to dread fear itself.

A week or so after that I first heard the whisper about the dog collar. They said Smith was wearing a dog's collar under his flannel shirt. The man who told me said it was a sign of insanity.

I didn't say anything, not to him. I did to Bertha.

"Wasn't that rubbing it in?" I asked.

She shrugged her massive shoulders. "It had to be something that would make him think more of his training than of himself. A man can get accustomed to a glove. He'll have the devil of a time getting accustomed to a dog collar."

"He'll lose his self-respect," I said.

"He ain't got any."

"The men will kid him about his collar."

"That'll make him remember what it's on there for. He's got to get in a fight before he's much better."

"He'll get an unmerciful licking."

"Of course, but after that he won't be afraid of a licking. And if the men know he'll fight, they won't pick on him so much."

"You may be a first-rate animal trainer," I told her, "but you can't pull that stuff with men."

She didn't even bother to contradict me. "We got some good roast beef," she said.

I was halfway through the meal when Fred Smith came in. He'd been in a fight that must have been a massacre. His lips were split, one eye was closed, the other was all puffed up. His shirt was torn and covered with dust. There was a trickle of red stains from his nose.

Big Bertha looked at him as though she saw nothing out of the ordinary. "We got some good roast beef," she said.

"Gimme an order," he lisped through his swollen lips.

She passed him over an order. His hands were trembling with excitement, and the fork jiggled a tune against the edge of the plate.

"Your dog's ready to come back," she said.

"Back?"

"Yes. Back to you. I've got him trained."

Smith drank a glass of water in big gulps and choked on the last gulp.

A man tapped me on the shoulder.

"Your name's Dunn?"

I nodded.

"Sam Flint wants to know if you can come to the mine right away. It's important."

I paid my check and followed the man to the dusty street. He had an automobile with the motor running. I got in, and the man snapped the gears home. We lunged forward in a swirl of dust. I noticed that several other cars were starting out in a great hurry.

"What's happened?" I asked the man at the wheel.

"Another payroll holdup."

"Did they get the roll?"

"Yes, and they got Ed Manse."

I said nothing more. Neither did the man. The facts could wait. Flint would want to tell them in his own way. Sam Flint was the main squeeze at the mine. He had been an old fighter, in the earlier days. Now he was getting along, but he could still fork a horse and pull iron.

He was pacing the rough board floor of the mining office when I came in.

"Dunn, you busted up some cattle rustlers down in New Mexico."

"I was in on some action there, yes."

"And they say you can read trail."

"I've read trail, some."

"All right. You're employed as special investigator by the mine. I want action. Also, there's a two-thousand-dollar reward for the arrest and conviction of the man or men who pulled the job."

"What job?"

"Murder, robbery. They got Ed Manse. I'm going out. Got some shooting irons along?"

"I could use an extra one."

He gave me a Winchester and an old single-action Colt, one of the kind you draw mostly by the hammer. It shot a bullet that did violent things to a human being.

"Let's go," he said.

The afternoon sun was slanting purple shadows along the ridges. It stays light pretty late up in those altitudes in the middle of summer. The hot wind had died down. The horizons had quit their heat dance of midday and were showing steady.

We jolted along the truck road, then swung out on a twisting dirt road that runs toward the Las Vegas highway. After five or six miles we came to a little knot of men, a couple of automobiles, and something stretched out on the ground, the face covered by a blanket.

Dead men are pretty gruesome, no matter how you take them. A man who has been shot in the heat of the day on the desert is something a man with a weak stomach has no business looking at. The red had baked black in the hot sun, where it had oozed over the little rocks that lay on the surface of the desert. Flies buzzed around in angry circles. The blanket was swarming with them.

Sam Flint strode toward the still form. Nick Cryder pulled back the blanket.

"He put up a battle," said Cryder.

That much was evident. There were tracks all around in the sand, places where feet had dug deep. Manse had got some bruises on his face before the shot had torn away the top of his head. There were two other bullet wounds, one in his chest, one just over the belt buckle. His gun was gone.

Sam Flint read signs on the ground just as though he had been reading a printed page.

"Lone bandit," he said. "Blocked the road, got the drop, made Manse stop the car and get out. Took his gun away, and then reached for the bag. Manse tackled him. The bandit clubbed his gun, cracked him on the face. Then he shot him in the shoulder. Manse kept on. The next shot caught him in the stomach. Manse fell back. The shot that did things to his head was fired after he lay back on the ground."

Nick Cryder nodded. "That's the way I dope it."

Sam Flint met his gaze steadily.

"Dusty Dunn's going to do some special investigation for us on this thing. There's a two-thousand-dollar reward."

Nick Cryder tilted back the brim of his hat. The setting

sun made little ridges and valleys in the tanned skin of his face.

"You haven't got full confidence in me?" he asked. His tone was as hard as his eyes.

Flint met his eyes. "No," he said, "I haven't."

Cryder turned to me: "Well, I'll tell you a few things. You've been hostile before, Dunn. You can guard anything you want, but you can't start out making arrests, and you can't start out trying to run down any criminals. That stuff is my business. What's more, you can't wear a gun unless you're a deputy."

He made a step toward me, then stopped.

"The law says I can wear a gun when I'm going on a hunting trip or returning from one," I said, "if you're wanting to get technical."

"That ain't got anything to do with it. You can't strut around here as a special officer, without authority."

I smiled at him. "I'm going on a hunting trip. Just starting."

Cryder thought things over for a minute. Then he turned to Flint:

"All right! But don't interfere with me—I've got the man spotted. Fred Smith drifted in here from Los Angeles. He's wanted there. His real name is Fred Gates. There's a forgery and embezzlement warrant out for him. I'm on his trail. He knows it. And he's wearing a few bruises; he's the one that did the job. I'm the first to tell you about it, and that means I get the reward."

Flint shook his white locks back from the perspiration on his forehead. "You arrest the right man and get a conviction, and you get the reward."

I looked around at the tracks. They had been messed up a little. There were powder burns around the bullet hole in the shoulder and the one that had taken off the top of his head. There were no powder burns around the hole in his stomach. That bullet had gone through from an angle.

I walked off into the desert, poking around.

The sun set. The Funeral Range showed a jagged silhouette against the sky. Breathless silence gripped the desert.

"What are you doing out there?" shouted Cryder.

"Walking," I called back.

"Come help us load the body."

I pretended I didn't hear him. After the sun once sets, it gets dark in that country pretty fast, and I wanted to find what I was looking for.

They had the body loaded and the car started before I found it. It was behind a little clump of greasewood, a place where someone had stretched out at full length. I looked around the ground. There was the glitter of a brass tube, a single empty cartridge thrown out from a rifle. I smelled it. It was fresh.

I followed the man's trail back to the automobile road. The man who had ambushed himself there had left the automobile that had figured in the holdup, walked diagonally across the desert, and tucked himself in behind the greasewood.

Sam Flint came over to where the trail met the road.

"Find something?"

"Yes. There were two of 'em," I pointed out. "When Manse was held up he only saw the lone man in front of him. There was another here in ambush. Manse watched his chance and tackled the man with the gun. He tore his mask off.

"The man behind the greasewood turned loose and caught him in the stomach. The other fellow managed a shot in the shoulder. Those two shots put Manse on his back, dying. The third shot was because he wasn't dying fast enough. The only reason it was necessary was because he'd seen the face of the man who stopped him and asked for the cash. He tore off the mask—you can see where the cord cut the skin on his fingers. He must have given it a big yank."

Sam Flint stroked his chin. His eyes were staring at me through the gathering dusk.

"Any idea who they were?"

"I'd like to see Harry Fane, on a hunch," I told him, "and see if there isn't a welt along the back of his head, such a welt as might be made by the cord when a mask is torn off."

"And the man behind the greasewood?"

I shrugged my shoulders. But we both turned toward Nick Cryder.

They took the body back to town. There was lots of excitement. I hunted up Big Bertha.

"Who had Fred Smith been fighting with?"

"He didn't say."

"Where did he go?"

"Don't know. He left before he'd eaten much, took the dog and beat it. Too excited to eat, I guess."

I kept watching her, waiting for her to raise her eyes to mine. She didn't do it.

"Maybe someone said something about the holdup and murder about the time he left?"

She kept her eyes on the floor for a second, then raised them to mine.

"You're a fool!" she spat at me, but the words lacked conviction. I could see there was a doubt in her mind.

I started up the trail back of the mine, the one that led to Fred Smith's shack. It was dark now, save for the stars and the curl of a new moon that hadn't yet reached the first quarter.

I could hear the sound of my feet crunching along the gravel, and then I stepped into the sand of the desert. The sand gave forth little whispering noises. The hills drew together, and then I came out in the little valley. There was a light in the house. I could see shadows moving across the light.

There were five men there: Cryder, Fane, and three cronies. Cryder had a black bag. It was splotched with red and was empty. He held it up before him and pointed out the red stains to the others. Fred Smith was not there.

I turned to go back. There was talk of lynching. The

men in the cabin behind me were cursing and making threats.

I figured Smith hadn't returned down the trail; he'd kept on up the valley. So I circled the cabin and started up the slithering sand of the valley floor.

It was a barren valley, surrounded by mountains that were baked slopes of colored stone. Here and there a clump of sage or greasewood, at times a stunted cactus. The moon was low, the stars were giving a little light. The mountains cut the sky with a wall of silence.

I wondered if Smith knew.

After a while I saw the beam of a flashlight cut the dark behind me. The manhunt was on. The two who had done the crime were ready to pin it on to the man who hadn't. And they planned that he would never be able to deny it. My only chance was to keep between that posse and its quarry. I wondered if the other three men knew the plot or were just dupes.

Of course, I had no proof—only the knowledge that there had been two men in the holdup; that Manse had been killed because he had seen a face. The whole thing hinged on the man behind the greasewood, he who had fired from ambush.

I came to the slope of the mountains and whistled a note of warning.

"Smith!" I called. "Oh, Fred Smith! It's Dusty Dunn."

There was no answer, no echo. The desert swallows up sounds like that. Behind me I could hear the posse. They were coming fast; their flashlights helped them make time.

I knew they'd be likely to take a shot at me if they saw me. I gave one more low call for Smith, but there was no answer. I hoisted myself up onto a ridge, stretched along an outcropping of rock that was still warm from the heat of the day, and waited.

They didn't see my tracks at all—going it blind. When they came to the mountains they split up into two parties.

Harry Fane and Nick Cryder came up my side of the canyon. I could hear them talking.

"You've got to watch out for Dusty Dunn." It was Fane's voice.

"He's not going to start anything," said Cryder.

Fane snorted. "Shows all you know about it! He's been snooping around and found out where someone lay out behind the greasewood and took a shot at Manse."

"How do you know?"

"That's what Sam Flint told someone."

"Wait a minute. We better think this one over some," said Cryder. "That complicates matters."

"That's what I was telling you."

They came to a stop and Fane did a lot of talking, while Cryder was thinking.

"We gotta be mighty careful," Fane finished. "Flint says Dusty Dunn knows Manse tore off a mask, and—"

A rock rattled.

"Somebody up that ridge!" Cryder yelled, and jumped forward. A dog barked. Cryder cast the beam from his flashlight up the dark slope. For a moment the beam groped against the side of the hill, then it picked up the green eyes of a dog. The beam shifted a bit, and there was Fred Smith.

"I heard you," he said. "You two were the stickups."

I pinched myself. Was this Fred Smith, coming out of hiding and walking straight toward two armed murderers who would have to kill him to protect themselves?

He came on toward them. Cryder fired. The bullet spat into the ground; it had missed Smith by inches. Smith tried to dodge, lost his footing, and came rolling down the slope. The dog sprang forward, yellow teeth gleaming.

As Fane fired the second time I got into action and took a shot at the flashlight. I missed it, but the cross fire made them jump for cover.

And then the dog connected. He went for Fane's throat in a spring that made him thud against Fane's chest with a jar and sent them both crashing to the earth.

Fred Smith was running straight and low like a football player, coming for Nick Cryder. And Nick Cryder was taking deliberate aim. He wasn't going to miss this time.

I hated to interfere, but Smith was running into lead. I had a good chance to get Cryder's hip as it was silhouetted against the beam of the flashlight, and I fired. The shot bowled him over just as Fred Smith tackled.

There were shouts; men came on the run. I stood on the ridge and held them back. Smith and the dog did their stuff in the canyon below. It was all over in a few seconds; they were lively seconds, too. Cryder's cronies were hostile, but I kept my guns in my hands and we all went back to town together.

Cryder had to be carried. Fane was frightened more than hurt. He'd managed to hold his arms in front of his face when the dog jumped, and his arms had been pretty badly chewed up.

After we got to town there wasn't much left to do. We found the payroll buried back of Cryder's shack. He'd planted the bag at Smith's cabin. The town was pretty talkative all night, and Fane made a confession. He tried to put all the blame on Cryder.

But Cryder was able to show that he was the man behind the greasewood brush. That meant that Fane had fired the fatal shot, the one that had lifted Manse's skull. That was because Manse had seen Fane's face behind the black mask.

When the excitement died down we found that Fred Smith was something of a hero. Sam Flint doubled the reward and split it between Fred and me. I thought of what Cryder had said about Smith being really Fred Gates, wanted in Los Angeles, but I didn't say anything. I'd been employed to get the bandits. Flint could do the broadcasting.

Fred Smith disappeared the next afternoon. He just faded from town, and Big Bertha and the dog went with him. No one knew when they'd gone, or where. They simply weren't around.

I didn't hear of them for more than two months. Then I got a marked copy of the Los Angeles *Times*. The article blocked out with a pencil was quite brief.

On its face it contained little of interest, merely reported the criminal trial of three directors of some corporation. They had been convicted of embezzlement, alteration of records, and forgery.

The article said that the directors had originally placed the blame on the assistant manager, who had become panic-stricken and fled, although innocent. He had felt that his word against that of three directors would not be accepted. But he had returned, faced the charges and the lying directors, demanded an investigation, fought the case to a conclusion, and uncovered evidence which had exposed the conspiracy.

The name of the assistant manager was Fred Gates. The article mentioned that he had assumed the name of Fred Smith following his abrupt departure from the city.

They had never returned to the Armagosa country. The old prospector's cabin is deserted; the wind whips the sand against the sides of the unpainted shack, and the sand hisses little whispers. It seems as though the old house and the drifting sand are whispering together about the gossip of the desert country.

I've heard it many a time, and I wonder if the old shack doesn't tell the drifting sand the story of the man who conquered the lesser fears and then tackled the big fear.

Crooked Lighting

Bob Fairfield strolled from the taxicab to the train gate at the Southern Pacific depot in San Francisco with that subtle something in his manner which indicated a seasoned traveler. There was nothing in his expression or in his bearing to indicate that a small fortune in diamonds reposed in the light handbag which he was very particular to keep only in his left hand.

Casually he exhibited his ticket to Los Angeles, strolled past the gateman and down the long line of dark Pullmans. His eyes flicked to the car numbers, posted on bits of pasteboard in the windows. At car eleven he resisted the efforts of the porter to take charge of the handbag, called out the number of his berth, and entered.

It lacked precisely eighty seconds of the time the gate would clang shut, one hundred and forty seconds of the time the powerful locomotive would pull out the long line of heavy cars.

Nearly all the passengers had boarded the train. The odd-numbered berths were made up. The even-numbered side of the car contained a sprinkling of passengers.

Bob Fairfield flashed a glance of swift appraisal and sighed.

"Travel's light," he muttered, removed his raincoat and hat, tossed them behind the green curtains of lower seven, and dropped into the seat across the aisle. The bag was still in his hand and he used it for an armrest.

His eyes flicked up and down the car, then suddenly came to a halt. Bob Fairfield edged a little more toward the end of the seat so he could get a better look at the man who had just entered the car.

Slick Simms, the smoothest gem man on the coast, was standing in one corner, near the vestibule, his eyes wandering up and down the car.

Fairfield placed Simms instantly, and instantly became guarded in his motions. His right hand surreptitiously patted the butt of the pistol which hung in a shoulder holster beneath his left armpit. He sat erect, watchful, ready for instant action.

As the junior partner of a firm dealing almost exclusively in choice diamonds, Bob Fairfield knew the more prominent crooks who specialized in gems. And he knew Slick Simms particularly and most unfavorably. Yet, he felt sure, Simms didn't know him. Bob's inspection of the crook had been from behind the screen in a room at the police station. The officers had paraded Simms up and down that room, and more than a dozen important gem dealers had observed him carefully.

The police hadn't been able to get the goods on Slick Simms. They were morally certain of more than twenty crimes which Simms had engineered. But they had not one whit of evidence against him.

Bob Fairfield crossed to his berth, crawled behind the curtains, and, from that point of vantage, surveyed the car. He was accustomed to carrying thousands of dollars in gems with him. Ordinarily he took precautions against the more crude forms of holdup. He kept well in the beaten paths of travel and minded his own business.

In five years he had not experienced a single loss. And he had become somewhat scornful of the power of crooks. Mechanically he kept his gun within reaching distance, habitually carried his bag in his left hand, and never made acquaintances on the train. Aside from these simple precautions, he traveled as any other man might travel.

He thought of dropping off and taking a later train. The Whitney diamonds were well worth the personal attention of Slick Simms. And the presence of the crook made Fairfield nervous. But the clanging of the engine bell, the creaking of the Pullmans, the slamming of vestibule doors, advised him he was too late.

Beyond a brief stop at San Jose, the train would run straight through the night. Then would come a stop at Santa Barbara, a pause for water at Somis, and the Arcade Station at Los Angeles. To leave the train at San Jose would necessitate a long wait and a slower train. Fairfield shrugged his shoulders and decided to see it through.

Simms walked down the slightly swaying aisle and dropped into the seat Fairfield had just vacated. There was about him a stealthy catlike motion that suggested a stalking animal. But he was careful not even to flash a glance at the berth across the way. In fact, his cold, gray eyes seemed to find the tips of his folded fingers of supreme interest.

The train gathered momentum. Sheets of rain dashed against the windows. Wind howled over the steel roof of the car. But the locomotive purred into the storm with constantly increasing acceleration.

Fairfield flashed a glance at the other passengers. A swift appraisal indicated that not even all the lower berths in the car were sold. The sudden storm had caused a last-minute cancellation of reservations, and not over eight or nine persons were in the car.

Simms sighed, tilted back his head, and in turn made a swift survey of the car. He seemed utterly unconscious of Bob Fairfield's intent gaze. Rather, his own interest seemed to be at the other end of the car. A girl in lower twelve held the cold interest of the gray eyes for a second or two, then Simms once more dropped his lids, and the tips of his folded fingers again became of paramount importance.

The Pullman conductor appeared in the vestibule and

started down the aisle, collecting tickets. Behind him came the train conductor.

Bob Fairfield slipped from his berth, still carrying his bag, and approached the Pullman conductor.

"Let me have a word with you right away, please," Bob said, and walked into the vacant drawing room at the end of the car.

The Pullman conductor paused, let his shrewd eyes flash over the gem dealer's face, then followed.

"We're taking tickets now," he said. "Unless it's very urgent you'd better wait—"

Bob kicked the door shut, grinned, and sat down.

"It's urgent," he said. "I'm Fairfield, of Sutter, Madison and Fairfield, diamond brokers. I've got a small fortune in gems in this bag. There are half a dozen prospective customers in Los Angeles, and I'm going to conclude a deal with one or the other of them tomorrow.

"You've got a crook in the car who specializes in diamonds. It may be just a coincidence, but I'm taking no chances. I want to cancel out of lower seven and get a drawing room, preferably in another car."

The conductor let his gimlet eyes take in every detail of Fairfield's appearance, then nodded.

"All right. I get your point. But this is the only vacant drawing room I'm sure of. I'll take your tickets now so you won't be disturbed during the night. You can lock the door. But it'll cost you another railroad ticket and more Pullman fare."

Bob pulled out a roll of bills, peeled off a crisp yellow-backed one, and nodded.

"Fix me up right now if you can. I want that door locked."

"Rather risky carrying gems on a train, ain't it?" asked the conductor as he made out a cash receipt.

Fairfield smiled. "I've carried millions of dollars' worth back and forth and haven't had a loss yet. That's only half of the story. I don't propose to have a loss. It's not really risky. After all, there's probably no one who knows in advance where I'm going or when. I keep my business to myself and don't take chances. This crook outside couldn't have followed me to the train, and I don't see how he could have learned I was going south tonight, not unless there's a leak in our own office. But he won't break into this drawing room, and he won't get a chance to grab my bag and drop off the train, so I'm not worrying. But I'll feel better behind a locked door than behind buttoned curtains."

The official smiled, nodded, and extended change and receipt.

"All right, Mr. Fairfield. Good night."

The door slammed. Fairfield shot the bolt. The train roared its way through the storm-filled night.

After the gem dealer had made certain arrangements he rang for the porter, had his berth made up, gave instructions that he was not to be disturbed, and as the porter left, stood for a moment in the doorway.

IF Slick Simms was at all annoyed by the manner in which his quarry had eluded him, he gave no outward indication of the fact. His cold eyes were still fastened on the tips of his fingers. But, as Bob stood in the doorway, making a last survey of the situation without, the crook raised his eyes once more in a swift flicker of appraisal.

Bob noticed that the glance was not for him but, as it had been before, for the girl in lower twelve. Bob turned his own eyes to the girl, saw that she was uncommonly pretty, young, alert, yet seemed to emanate an atmosphere of keeping to herself. She was hardly one that a traveler would try to strike up a train acquaintance with.

Her seat faced the door of Bob's stateroom and he had an excellent opportunity to observe her face, the dark aura of black hair, the sweep of the long lashes, the full lips.

And then, as though feeling his eyes upon her, she looked up, swiftly, almost with alarm.

For a split second Bob looked into the depths of the

dark eyes, and then, before he could avert his own gaze, he saw the expression of the dark eyes change from curious interest to swift suspicion. There was something almost of fear in the eyes of the girl. A hand flashed to the vanity case in her lap.

And Bob Fairfield slammed the door of his stateroom.

One of his cardinal rules was never to speak to a woman on the train. But the suspicion in those eyes haunted him as he undressed. After all, why should she have looked at him in that manner? What was there about him to make the girl suspicious? And what could she possibly fear?

Then Fairfield thought of Slick Simms. Was it possible the crook was not on his own trail at all but was trailing the girl in lower twelve?

A dozen things clicked in Bob's mind. There was the interest Simms took in the girl, the fact that he had taken a seat across from Bob's berth, his lack of interest when Bob had transferred to a drawing room.

The girl was carrying something very valuable, perhaps a consignment of precious stones. Simms was trailing her. Surely he would not have been so crude as to have taken the seat across from Bob's berth had Bob Fairfield been the one he was trailing.

Bob thought of warning the girl, reached toward the brass doorknob, then shook his head and dropped his hand. After all, Bob's first duty was to his firm. Slick Simms was so resourceful the police could get nothing on him. He worked a modification of the confidence game for the purpose of gathering in his gems. If he ever resorted to violence, the police had never learned of it.

And Simms had earned his nickname of "Slick." He was resourceful, devilishly clever. After all, the girl might be a plant to get Bob's interest. That warning he would give might be the very thing Simms was planning on. The girl might be a confederate, would use the warning as an entering wedge.

Bob disrobed, donned his pajamas, and crawled into the berth. The girl in lower twelve would have to take her own chances with Simms. Bob Fairfield certainly wasn't going to violate a cardinal rule of conduct and butt into something that was none of his business. He had his own gems to watch. Let the girl take care of herself.

The train thundered on in the storm. The wheels clicked along the rails. The wind howled across the ventilators in the steel roof of the car. Rain streamed against the windows, and Bob slept, a smile of serene confidence on his face, his leather handbag tied firmly to his arm with a slender steel chain.

During the night there was not so much as a whisper of menace, not the slightest sound of exploring fingers testing the door of the drawing room.

Bob Fairfield slept late. When he stretched, yawned, and raised the shade the train had left Santa Barbara and was clipping along the famous Rincon. The blue waters of the Santa Barbara channel caught the golden rays of the early sun and sent them tossing back like sparkling diamonds.

Those rays caused Bob to reach hastily for his traveling bag. He fitted a key, opened it, took from the bottom a thick jewel case, snapped it open, and held it to the window.

The Whitney diamonds glittered back at him with a million coruscations of scintillating light.

Bob sighed, snapped the case shut, and dropped it in his bag.

He dressed, shaved, rang the bell, and ordered breakfast sent to his room. He was taking no chances. He had insured the safety of his precious gems by taking a drawing room, and he didn't intend to leave it until the train pulled into the Arcade Station.

It was when the waiter was thrusting the steaming tray through the open door that Bob caught his glimpse of the occupants of the car. There was the usual careless curiosity, the idle wonderment of travelers who have nothing in particular to occupy their attention and so make an enforced observation of their fellow travelers.

But there was more—there were two faces which impressed themselves upon Bob's mind.

The girl in lower twelve had evidently passed a sleepless night. Her eyes were red and swollen. Her face was white, the lips pale. But her stubborn little jaw was clenched with determination. Her right hand clutched the vanity case until the skin showed white over the knuckles. Her eyes were fastened upon Bob Fairfield, and this time there could be no mistaking the suspicious hostility that shone from their dark depths.

The second face that caught Bob's attention was that of Slick Simms. The crook had about him that air of a cat about to spring which gave to the cold eyes an expression of chilling menace. He had leaned slightly forward in his seat, and the gray eyes were staring at the back of the head that showed from lower twelve. It was as though he merely waited for the girl to leave her seat in order to pounce.

The porter had made up the car. Only one berth still was covered by green curtains. The passengers had, for the most part, returned from breakfast. And Bob Fairfield caught something in the expression of the girl's face that made him realize she had not breakfasted. Apparently she had neither eaten nor slept.

And then the smiling waiter set the tray on Bob's table, and the door slammed shut on the sight of those two faces.

Bob poured a cup of coffee, broke a roll, reached for a strip of crisp bacon, and shrugged his shoulders. Fairfield wouldn't have classified himself as being particularly selfish. But he was looking out for number one. And one of his rules was to keep away from other passengers.

Two hours passed. The train had crawled up the Santa Susana Pass, wound its way down the mountains of twisted rock, roared through the San Fernando Valley, and the sound of its bell took on a muffled resonance as it crept into the Arcade Station. The storm of the night before had evaporated under the magic of southern California skies, and the sun shone vividly from a blue-black sky that was innocent of the trace of a cloud.

Bob Fairfield deliberately waited until the other passengers had left the car. Then he stepped out into the balmy air, walked rapidly through the passenger tunnel, out to the street, and, as a matter of principle, turned down the first cab that solicited his patronage, picked the second, and was driven rapidly to his hotel.

He had sufficient business in Los Angeles to pay him to keep a room by the month at one of the modern hotels. And that room was like home to Bob Fairfield. In it he kept a supply of clean clothes, some favorite books, and a small but highly efficient safe. That safe was guaranteed to balk the efforts of a burglar for several hours at the very least.

Not that Fairfield expected to be held up in his room in a Los Angeles hotel; but he didn't care to carry his gems in his pocket whenever he went out, yet he needed to have them instantly available to show to customers. The hotel safe would have been satisfactory were it not for the delay incident to putting stones in and taking them out every time a prospect came to his room. And so Fairfield preferred to keep his own private safe in his room.

The clerk at the hotel was effusive in his greeting. The sunshine had warmed Bob's soul, his breakfast had been perfect, and the gem dealer felt very much at peace with the world.

He went to his room, spun the dials on the safe, swung the door open, took the Whitney diamonds from his bag, gave them a final inspection, set them in the safe, shut the door, and twirled the dials. Then he heaved a great sigh of relief. Despite the fact that he was inclined to smile at his suspicions of the night before, there was something about Slick Simms that gave him the creeps, a subtle emanation of impending menace, an ingenuity that transcended any ordinary measures of defense.

"Getting nervous," Fairfield muttered. He poured himself a drink from a bottle containing genuine prewar whiskey, swallowed it, and strolled to the door of his room. He wanted to run down for a chat with the manager of the hotel, look up an acquaintance for lunch, and then he would get in touch with his list of prospects and try to dispose of the diamonds.

In the corridor, as he turned to lock the door, he became conscious of a feminine figure rounding a corner in the hall and heading slowly for the elevator. But Fairfield gave her scant notice. He was not one to become interested in passing women, nor was he one to stare.

And then, suddenly, he heard a gasp, sensed the menace of swift motion, and caught the glint of light on metal.

The woman who stood, one hand to her breast, the other holding a small automatic leveled at his stomach, was the dark-eyed girl of lower twelve.

"I thought you were following me!" she exclaimed. "You're trying for my gems, eh? Well, my good man, I've seen enough. You'll have a chance to explain to the police."

Fairfield felt his jaw sag in surprise.

"What are you talking about? And point that thing the other way," he snapped.

Her jaw set with righteous determination. "You followed me to the train. You transferred to a drawing room so you could be near my berth. But I sat up all night and you didn't get a chance to rob me. So you followed me here and managed to get a room on the same floor.

"I see it all now. I had the right hunch when I discharged my secretary. The police told me she'd been seen with a gem thief. So she tipped you off to my hotel reservations as well as the number of my berth on the train, did she? Well, we'll see what the police have to say to you.

"March toward that elevator, and if you move your

hands I'll shoot. I'm going to take you right down to the lobby and turn you over to the house detective."

Suddenly the humor of the situation burst upon Fairfield, and he chuckled.

"You think *I'm* a gem thief?" he asked.

The flashing dark eyes sparkled with scorn.

"And don't think you can talk me out of it!" she flashed.

Bob Fairfield deliberately violated her injunction about moving his hands and extracted a card case from his waistcoat pocket. From it he took his card and handed it to her.

"Permit me. I'm Fairfield, of Sutter, Madison and Fairfield. We're diamond brokers. I keep this room in the hotel by the month. The management can give you all necessary confirmation."

The dark eyes widened. The gun dropped slowly, then vanished in the depths of the vanity case.

"For heaven's sake!" exclaimed the girl. "Why, I'm Grace Delano from Seattle. I've had business dealings with your firm. Good gracious! Bob Fairfield, and to think that I'd mistake you for a thief. Why, I've had letters from you this last month—"

She burst into a peal of laughter.

"But I was carrying some very valuable gems—you know the pearl necklace from the Potter collection. I have it here in my bag. There's a customer calling on me, and when you changed your berth for a drawing room—"

She thrust out a friendly hand. Fairfield took it and bowed formally.

"Look," she said.

She opened the vanity case, snapped open a side compartment, and Bob caught the glint of snowy pearls against the black leather.

"I've got an offer I think I'll accept on them," said the girl, glancing cautiously about her. And then, suddenly, the bag snapped shut.

A MAN was walking down the hall. He came with the soft, furtive tread of a stalking cat. His cold gray eyes were fixed upon Bob Fairfield and the girl in a stare that was filled with menace. Just behind him were two sinister characters. They might have been piano movers, stevedores, or thugs. They wore rather shabby clothes. Their hats were pulled low over eyes that glittered in the light that came from the end of the hall.

Bob recognized Slick Simms, the noted yet unconvicted gem thief, and simultaneously registered the deserted hallway in which no one was likely to intrude, the menacing figures, the girl, the pearls, his own helplessness.

"Quick, in here," he said.

And there was something in his tone that caused her to give instant obedience. Bob twisted the key in the lock of his door, flung it open, grasped the girl's arm, and thrust her in.

Slick Simms turned, gave a swift word to his two companions, and the three quickened their pace to almost a run. But Bob Fairfield, jerking the key from the lock, sprang inside the room, shot the bolt, and stood poised, listening.

The girl stared at him with her hand to her throat, her pale lips parted.

"What is it?" she asked.

Bob Fairfield frowned at her. "That's Slick Simms, the notorious gem thief. He followed you down here. He was on the same car with us. I saw him, and that's why I went into a drawing room. I was afraid he was after me. I had the Whitney diamonds in my bag."

The black eyes widened, then twinkled with humor. "And I never knew he was on the train, but I sat up all night because I was suspicious of *you!*"

Fairfield nodded. "But that watchfulness probably saved you from robbery. You say your secretary had been seen with a crook? See how easy it is? A girl in your office could tip off a crook. We all face that same danger. A leak as to what we're carrying, the reservation on the car

—and that's all a clever crook wants. Of course, I'm a man and can take my own chances. But you shouldn't carry valuable gems."

She motioned to the door. "He's waiting outside?"

"I don't know, but I'm going to have him locked up on suspicion anyhow."

He reached toward the telephone.

"Oh, no, please don't." The girl's tone was low, throaty, pleading. "You see, the papers would get hold of it. The client who's negotiating for the pearls wouldn't think of buying them for a minute it it was to get out. That's why I came myself. She wanted me to keep the entire matter in absolute confidence—but I don't want to be selfish. You have the Whitney diamonds to consider."

Bob Fairfield laughed. He was commencing to feel very much master of the situation, very proud of himself.

"Not me. I have a safe there that would take a crook a few hours with an acetylene torch to crack. I chuck my stones in there whenever I get in. It saves worrying about them."

Eager fingers pulled a glistening string of pearls from the bag.

"Could you—would you—that is, would it be asking too much—just for an hour or two?"

Bob reached for the string. A glance told him that it was genuine, almost priceless as pearls went.

"Not at all," he said. The very possession of such a string of pearls was sufficient to vouch for the girl's identity.

He stooped before the safe, twisted the dials, took out the case holding the diamonds, opened it, and dropped the pearls inside.

"I'm only too glad to accommodate you, Miss Delano, It's strange we've never met before. I was thinking of it the other day when I dictated you a bulletin asking for some stones to match an order. You've been up there two or three years, haven't you? My secretary said she knew you."

The girl nodded. "Three and a half years . . . Oh, say, let me see that string again. The clasp is bent. I wanted to fix it before my customer saw it."

Bob handed her the case, watched while she set it on a table, took out the pearls, and adjusted the catch with skillful fingers. Then she held the string to the light, let her eyes feast upon it for a moment, and glanced at the case.

"Oh, yes, the Whitney diamonds," she said, and appraised them with the eye of an expert.

She went to the window to get a better light, turned the gems over and over, then replaced them.

The telephone rang, a sharp, imperative summons. Fairfield answered and listened for a few moments.

"I don't care to see Mr. Simms," he barked into the mouthpiece, and hung up.

"Can you beat that? This crook, Simms, has the clerk telephone me that he's anxious to see me at once on a matter of the most urgent business."

The girl had a little tinkling laugh that rippled upon Bob's consciousness with a sensation of distinct pleasure.

"I should say he *would* like to see us right now! Well, I must be getting on. I'll drop in after lunch for the necklace, and I'm a thousand times obliged to you."

She gave him her hand, and Bob noticed the velvety smoothness of the creamy skin, noticed once more the expression of her dark eyes, and this time was pleased to see that suspicion had given way to something akin to admiration.

"You're no end clever, you know," she purred.

Bob's deprecatory gesture was more formal than otherwise.

She went out and Bob locked the safe, telephoned his prospects, and went out to lunch.

"Trusting little thing," he muttered to himself. "Think of leaving me that string of pearls without even so much as a receipt!"

At two thirty-five his first prospect called.

Bob served highballs, passed cigars, then went to the safe, opened it, and took out the jewel case. He turned his back to the prospect long enough to lift out the string of pearls and drop them in his pocket, then presented the case to the potential customer.

"The finest matched diamonds on the coast," he said.

The man nodded.

"Yes, yes, I know. I'm familiar with the reputation of the stones," he remarked, and took the case to the window.

There was a moment of silence, then a sudden, swift exclamation as sharply sibilant as the hissing of a sword in the air.

"Is this a joke?"

Bob, vaguely nettled at the tone, walked to the window.

"A joke? What do you mean? I'm not accustomed to—"

He broke off as the breath expelled from his lungs.

The stones that glittered in the light of the window were not the Whitney diamonds. They were better than a paste imitation. They were zircons. On their background of white cotton they sent back the light in varicolored scintillations. But to the eye of an expert they showed their true nature.

A cold sweat burst out on Fairfield's forehead.

He plunged his hand into his pocket and took out the string of pearls. They were the most flimsy of imitations. In a good light they showed up as nothing but beads.

"She tricked me!" yelled the dealer, and sprang for the telephone.

Two hours later when the police made their report, Bob Fairfield knew that he'd been stung.

"The real Grace Delano was found bound and gagged in an automobile in Sacramento," reported the police detective who had taken charge of the case. "She'd started out with a string of pearls from the collection of Sidney Potter. Crooks robbed her and got the pearls.

"But we've caught Slick Simms. He was just leaving the hotel when our men picked him up. I haven't had a chance to give him a work over yet, but I left word to have him brought up here."

There came a knock at the door. When Fairfield flung it open he was confronted by a policeman, the house detective, and the cold, expressionless eyes of Slick Simms, the ingenious crook on whom the police had not been able to fasten a charge.

"To whom am I indebted for this insult?" asked Simms in a quiet, ominous tone of voice. "My lawyer will want to know whom to make defendants in the suit I shall instruct him to bring for malicious arrest and persecution."

The detective laughed. "Yeah. But while you're talkin' you might as well tell us why you called up Mr. Fairfield here. The telephone call seems to have been most opportune, since your woman confederate managed to switch jewel cases while he was picking up the receiver."

Simms let his cold gray eyes flit from face to face in cautious scrutiny before he answered. Then he replied in a voice that was as expressionless as his face. It was as though he had rehearsed the scene many times.

"I was passing down the hall and saw this gentleman with the lady. It happened I knew the lady was Milly the Moll, the best little gem thief in the country. I thought he should be warned with whom he was associating. So I went to the lobby and had the clerk telephone, asking for permission to visit him in his room.

"That permission was refused in a manner that was most insulting, and if he has lost anything as a result of his discourtesy, I'm glad of it."

The detective looked at Fairfield. Fairfield looked at the detective.

"This way, sir," said the detective, motioning Fairfield into the hall.

"There ain't any use trying to bluff that baby," announced the detective, jerking his thumb toward the room. "I'll go ahead with it if you want, but we won't get anywhere, and he'll undoubtedly sue you if you sign a complaint for a warrant. He knows what he can do and what he can't do. He's always popping up with some new scheme. If he'd ever work the same one twice, we'd stand a chance of getting him. But he's always flashing a brand-new one on us.

"Down in the department we call him Crooked Lightning, because he never strikes twice in the same place."

Fairfield took a deep breath and clenched his fists. "Now that you've caught him, you mean to say you're going to let him go?"

The detective shrugged his shoulders. "If you want to sign a complaint, go to it. But maybe you'd better see a lawyer first. After all, what have you got on him? He rode down on the train, called you on the telephone, as he says, to warn you."

Fairfield passed a hand over his clammy brow. A succession of thoughts whirled through his mind.

"But can't you trace his moves for the past few days, link him with the girl?"

The detective laughed, a short, ugly laugh. "I'd give six months' salary to convict him, but we've traced his back trail before. That's why they call him Slick Simms. You won't find a thing. And the next time he strikes he'll have a brand-new scheme, played in a different way."

Fairfield turned back toward the room and flung the door back.

"Get out!" he snapped at the gray-eyed crook.

"And you might fire your secretary, or whoever knew of your trip and arranged your Pullman reservations," suggested the detective.

Slick Simms paused in mid-stride, halfway to the door.

"I doubt if it's worthwhile—now," he remarked, "if you'll pardon my intruding the suggestion. You see, lightning never strikes twice in the same place."

And, with that, he had bowed himself into the corridor

and was gone, his tread as swiftly furtive as that of a stalking cat.

Fairfield turned to the detective and suddenly chuckled.

"Damned if I don't admire the man's nerve!" he exclaimed. "He knows you'd get him if he ever got mixed up in two of the same sort of schemes."

The detective nodded. But his lips did not share Fairfield's smile. His eyes glowed with smoldering hatred.

"Some day he'll make the mistake of resisting arrest," he half muttered.

But Fairfield continued to smile. "Not that bird. I believe he enjoys it. But I'm immune. You say he never strikes twice in the same place. And let's be thankful for that."

From the corridor sounded the clang of the elevator door as Slick Simms, Crooked Lightning, left to embark upon a fresh adventure.

At Arm's Length

THE rain which had started in as a drizzle the afternoon before had turned into a downpour during the night and was still hanging on as a cold, steady barrage of raindrops which had spattered on the cuffs of Jerry Marr's trousers, soaked his shoes, and darkened the light tan of his raincoat.

Marr stood in front of the office door, fitting a key to the lock with cold, wet fingers. He shot the bolt, opened the door, and switched on the lights, disclosing what had once been a single room, now divided by a wood and frosted glass partition into a cubbyhole reception room with a private office beyond.

Jerry stooped to pick up his mail. There were two letters, both addressed to Jerry Marr, Special Investigator. Water dripped down from Marr's hatbrim as he studied the envelopes. They were both the side-flap which simulated first-class, private mail, yet which could be sent out at half the cost.

Jerry scaled them both into the wastebasket without bothering to open them. He removed his hat and shook water from the brim by giving it a quick, downward jerk. He hung the hat on the brass hook by a diamond-shaped mirror, squirmed broad shoulders out of his raincoat, took a folded newspaper from the side pocket, hung up the coat, and went into the inner office to read about the murder of Elaine Dixmer.

Others might read through morbid curiosity, might roll the spicy morsel of suggested scandal over their tongues. Marr read for business reasons. There was nothing relaxed in his posture, nothing indolent about him. His elbows placed on the desk, his hands holding the moist pages of the newspaper flat before him, he read in frowning concentration.

When he had finished reading, he pushed the cheap, squeaky swivel chair back from the narrow desk, got up, and walked over to look out of the window at the rain beating down on the glass skylight of a restaurant two floors below. After a few moments he spun around on his heel and walked back to the swivel chair and the newspaper. He turned the pages, carefully studying every item dealing with crime news.

On the fourth page his eye caught a headline: TACK SPRINKLER AT WORK IN HYDE PARK DISTRICT.

Marr narrowed his eyes in thoughtful concentration as he read the brief paragraph announcing that a mysterious tack sprinkler, who had during the past week scattered large roofing tacks at various places on the highways, had again been at work in the Hyde Park district. A motorist had reported that he had encountered a man with a broom sweeping tacks from the highway there. The motorist had reported to the police because he had failed to notice any automobile parked nearby and had therefore assumed that the person sweeping up the tacks might have been a resident nearby who had voluntarily assumed the task of clearing the highway.

Inasmuch as police had received no complaints, the matter had been filed for routine investigation.

Marr, who believed that the most significant clues consisted of isolated facts, seemingly insignificant in themselves, noted the name and address of the motorist. A search of the telephone directory gave him the man's number, and Marr put through the call. A woman answered the telephone.

"Automobile Club," Marr said. "Can I speak with the

man who reported finding tacks in the Hyde Park district?"

Shortly thereafter a man's voice came over the wire. "This is Clyde Trimble. What is it you wanted to know?"

"Exactly where did you encounter those tacks?" Marr asked.

"I didn't encounter them," Trimble explained. "It was raining, and I saw a man standing in the road. I slowed down and swung to one side, thinking it was a holdup. The man had a broom and was sweeping tacks off the highway. He motioned me to go ahead. I thought at first he was from the Auto Club. Later on, I remembered I hadn't noticed any car parked nearby, so I telephoned the police. They didn't do anything about it."

"That was Tuesday night?"

"Yes."

"Exactly where was it in the Hyde Park district?"

"I don't know," Trimble said. "It was some place on Belton Drive."

"Do you remember the time?"

"Not exactly. It was right around nine o'clock."

"Can you give me a description of the man?" Marr asked.

"No, I can't. You know how it is at a time like that. It was raining, and I was in a hurry. I'd been coming in on the through highway from Centerville. I can take a shortcut by turning off at Garver Way, climbing up to the summit, and coming down through the Hyde Park district. It's closer that way to where I live."

"This was on Belton Drive?"

"That's right. Just about at the foot of the grade before you come to Olive Street."

Marr said, "Okay. We're investigating," and hung up before Trimble could make any embarrassing inquiries.

A check of the city map showed that the point mentioned was not far from the house in which Elaine Dixmer had been murdered. Because police received dozens of minor complaints which were handled as a matter of routine and delegated to various departments, the significance, if any, had for the moment escaped them.

But Jerry Marr, who had more time than the police and a much greater curiosity, turned over in his mind the significance of a possible connection, although as yet, even to his imaginative mind, there seemed to be no reason to believe that a man sweeping tacks from the highway could have any connection with a murder. Jerry, however, realized that it was highly unusual for a citizen to have such a philanthropic interest in the welfare of his fellow motorists that he would set out in a driving rain to sweep tacks from a highway.

He once more pushed back his chair, got to his feet, lit a cigarette, and stood staring at nothing. His thoughtful eyes looked far beyond the drab walls of his gloomy little office. His imagination—a quality which he claimed was woefully lacking so far as police investigations were concerned—was busily at work.

Abruptly he ground out the cigarette, strode out to the narrow oblong of the reception room, and picked up a card with a celluloid clock and two brass hands attached to it. The card had a sign saying OUT. WILL RETURN ABOUT.

Marr set the hands of the clock to ten-thirty, put on his damp hat and wrestled his shoulders into the raincoat, switched off the lights, hung the sign on the front of the door, and went out into the rain.

He kept his battered flivver in a parking lot across from the building. The attendant, seated in a little shelter, the windows of which were steamy with condensation from the heat of a gas stove, recognized Marr and nodded in the general direction of Marr's car.

Jerry splashed through little puddles of water, opened the door of the car, rattled the motor into life, turned on a dispirited windshield wiper which did more smearing than wiping, and drove the car out into traffic.

Belton Drive twisted away from Olive Street to wind up a deep cleft between two hills. In the sullen rain it looked like a glistening, wet serpent snaking its way down from the canyon. Back of this canyon, the steep, southern California mountains rose to meet the leaden clouds which hung ominously black and motionless less than a thousand feet above the little bungalows which perched precariously on the slopes above Belton Drive.

Jerry Marr shifted his car into second gear and climbed steadily. The house where Elaine Dixmer had been murdered showed bleak and desolate in the rain. In the newspapers it had been described as "an exotic love nest." Seen in the wet daylight, it looked as drab and lifeless as the dining room of a nightclub at nine o'clock in the morning.

There were two cars parked in front of the place. One of them had a press sign pasted on the windshield. The other one was a private car of the type driven by those who regard first cost as a determining factor.

Marr swung his car in a U-turn, dropped back down to a point fifty yards below the house, and parked the car, leaving it in gear. Then he pulled his hat down low on his forehead, got out, and started sloshing down the road through the rain.

He had gone less than fifty yards when his eye caught the glint of metal. A pile of extra-long, large-headed roofing tacks had been swept from the edge of the pavement to a little depression near the side of the road.

Marr stood looking down at the pile of tacks for a moment, then stepped out into the soft, muddy soil and slid down the steep slope of a clay embankment to a place where little clumps of brush dotted the soggy, straw-colored, dried grass which had been baked during the long summer's dry season.

Marr prowled and poked around in the brush. His feet were sopping wet. Water oozed from the soaked leather with every step. The rain beat a muffled tattoo on his hatbrim and ran into little rivulets down the sides of his raincoat.

At length he found what he was looking for, a soggy box of grayish cardboard with a white label pasted on one end: *Extra-Large Roofing Tacks.* By holding the label on a slant so that light from the overcast sky reflected against it at just the right angle, Marr was able to detect the faint trace of a cost mark written in code and a selling price in figures.

Taking care not to rub any of the glazed surface from the wet label, Marr folded the box, pushed it down in the pocket of his raincoat, and scrambled up the slippery bank to the road. He walked back to his parked automobile, climbed inside, and coasted down the inclined road, throwing the car into gear and switching on the ignition when he had gathered enough momentum to start the motor.

Half a mile farther on, a residential building sat back from the road just far enough to make room for a wooden shed and two gasoline pumps between the house and the highway. Marr drove in under the shed and pressed his horn button.

A man in his forties emerged from the house, saying, "H'ryuh. Can I fill it up?"

Marr said, "Put in five, and check the oil and water."

He opened the car door, slid out to the wet gravel, and said, "Some rain."

"Uh-huh. We needed it."

"Had a murder up the road Tuesday night, didn't you?"

"Uh-huh."

"Police got any clues?"

"I don't think so."

"Fix any flats Tuesday night?"

The man quit pumping gasoline to look at Marr sharply. "Why?" he asked.

"Just wondered."

The man resumed his pumping of gasoline without answering the question.

"Nice place you have here."

"Uh-huh."

"Keep open nights?"

"Until about ten o'clock."

Marr took a ten-dollar bill from his pocket, folded it, and drew it back and forth through his fingers. When the man had finished putting gas in the tank, Marr handed him the ten. "No use monkeying with the windshield in weather like this," he said.

He counted his change carefully, put it in his pocket, and then said, "I want to find out about the man who had the flats fixed here Tuesday night.

"What about him?"

"What kind of a car was he driving?"

"Why do you want to know?"

Marr said, "I'm from the Automobile Club. Somebody was sprinkling tacks across the road. I've got the box they came in. I want to find someone who can make a complaint."

"Why didn't you say so in the first place?" the man asked. "I got his license number. His left front and his right rear both went flat about a hundred yards up the road. I walked up yesterday but couldn't find anything."

"You didn't go far enough," Marr said. "It takes a little while for a good tire to go down after a tack runs into the casing. Did this chap know you took his number?"

"No. I told him I thought he should make a squawk, but he didn't want to, said there was no use. There's been some of that tack-laying going on, you know."

"I'll say there has," Marr agreed. "I'd like to get this man's name."

"I can't give you his name, only the license number of his car. I jotted it down just in case."

"Let's have it," Marr said, making the request sound casual.

The man went in, opened the cash register, took out an oblong of soiled white paper on which a number had been written, and handed it to Marr. Marr opened his notebook and dropped it inside.

The man stood for a moment, ill at ease, then blurted, "I want that back. You can copy it."

"Oh, sure," Marr said, "but you won't have any more use for it. I'll handle the thing from now on."

The man remained obstinately silent, so Marr opened his notebook, pulled out a fountain pen, copied the license number into the notebook, then handed back the oblong slip of paper. "Pretty nice place here," he said.

"Uh-huh."

"I've been looking for a little place like this, a place where I could have my home, carry on my business, and sell a little gasoline on the side."

"Your business?" the man asked.

"Uh-huh. A mail order business," Marr said.

The man thought for a moment, then said, "Henderson's my name. I could let you have this place."

Marr said, "Glad to know you, Henderson. My name's Marr. How much?"

"Well, I don't know. I ain't exactly put a price on it yet. I make a pretty good living right out of this gasoline pump, and then having this place here, my rent don't cost me nothing and . . ."

"Tell you what you do, Henderson," Marr said. "Think it over. Figure out how much you want for the place. When you do, let me know, and—"

"Three thousand dollars," Henderson interrupted.

Marr cocked a thoughtful eye at the buildings. "Pretty much money," he said.

"You ain't even seen the inside of the house yet, mister."

Marr laughed. "I ain't even seen the three thousand yet."

Henderson joined in the laugh and said, "I wouldn't sell at all only I want to get into a climate that ain't so dry."

"It doesn't seem dry today," Marr said.

Henderson grinned affably and agreed that there was nothing dry about the day.

"Would you consider twenty-five hundred cash?" Marr asked.

Henderson surveyed him with shrewd, glittering eyes. "Hell," he said, "I believe you really *want* the place."

"I might at that," Marr said.

"How'd you know it was for sale?"

"I didn't. I'm looking for a good location."

"You know the game?" the man asked.

"Some," Marr said.

"Better come in and look the place over. If you want a good location, this is it."

"Get any regular trade from the places up the drive?" Marr asked.

"No."

Marr said easily, "Well, I'll keep the place in mind. It's more than I wanted to pay. If I don't find anything that looks good, I'll get in touch with you later."

Marr saw that the man's face was peering out at the license number of his automobile. For a moment Henderson stared through the window above the cash register, then his lips moved as he repeated the numbers, and Marr could follow the motions of his shoulder as he wrote down each of the numbers.

MARR pushed his way through the swinging doors which bore the name of Frank W. Gost. The customers' room was all but deserted, with its green leather chairs facing the blackboard on which, from time to time, sales and prices were posted. Marr didn't even notice the blackboard. His wet shoes squished at every step as he approached a counter behind which a telephone operator and a stenographer were busily engaged.

At the arch-shaped window marked Information, the telephone operator looked up expectantly.

Marr paused. "Mr. Gost," he said. "Take in my card."

He took a leather cardcase from his pocket, withdrew a plain, printed business card, and handed it to the girl.

"Did you have an appointment?" she asked, glancing dubiously at the stenographer.

"No," Marr said. "Take in my card."

"I'll tell him you're calling if you wish to explain what—"

"Take him my card," Marr said, "or I'm going to walk in."

The girl passed the card over to the stenographer. She took it, vanished through a swinging door, and after a few moments returned to say icily, "Mr. Gost doesn't place you, Mr. Marr. If you'll kindly tell me the nature of the business . . ."

Marr said, "Hell! I'm going in anyway."

Frank Gost, seated behind a big walnut desk, looked up in annoyance as Marr pushed his way through the door. He was in his late forties, with yellowish blond hair and protruding blue eyes. Reddish, swollen veins had wound angry little rivulets of inflammation across the whites of the eyes, but the man himself was big, aggressive, and dynamic. "Get the hell out of here," he said.

Marr drew up a chair and sat down.

Gost picked up the telephone and said into the transmitter, "Send Johnson in here."

When he had slammed the receiver back into place, Marr said casually, "You're in a spot."

Gost stared at him in silent hostility, then, picking up some correspondence from his desk, made as though to ignore the unwelcome visitor.

Marr said, "You're in a spot. It's going to be worth something to get off that spot. That's my specialty. I can get you off."

"Blackmail?" Gost asked sarcastically.

"That's it," Marr said. "There's a chance the police may check up with the guy who runs the service station, but not much. Those birds framed it for blackmail. Probably they wanted to get rid of her as badly as you did.

You're congratulating yourself that Elaine Dixmer is out of the way. You haven't seen anything yet. Wait until they start blackmailing you for murder."

Gost had been holding a letter in his hand. His fingers opened enough to let the letter slip down to the desk. His wide blue eyes stared incredulously at Marr. "Who—Who the devil are you?" he asked.

Marr said, "Special investigator. Call it a private detective if you want. Business wouldn't come to me, so I had to go out after business."

Gost's voice indicated his suspicion. "Why wouldn't business come to you?" he asked.

"Same reason it won't come to anyone else," Marr said. "But get this straight, brother: No damned depression is going to lick me."

Gost said, "Interesting, I'm sure. If I had the faintest idea what you were talking about, I'd find it much more interesting."

Marr said, "Nuts."

A door opened abruptly. A big man on the threshold glanced with cold hostility at Jerry Marr and said to Frank Gost, "You wanted me?"

"No," Gost said. "It was a mistake. Get out, and close the door."

As Johnson silently withdrew, Gost picked up the telephone and said to the girl at the switchboard, "See that I'm not disturbed for a few minutes." He dropped the receiver back in place and said to Marr, "Not that it means anything. I just want to find out how much hop you've been smoking."

Marr said, "Have it your own way. It's your funeral. If you want to stall around, go ahead. If you hadn't known what I was talking about, you'd have kicked me out. I can't help you unless you put your cards on the table."

Gost's red-rimmed eyes stared balefully at the detective. "If you think I'm going to put any cards on the table until I see more of your hand," he said, "you're crazy."

Marr thought for a minute, then said, "That sounds reasonable. Elaine Dixmer was murdered about nine o'clock Tuesday night out back of Belton Drive. A neighbor heard a scream, saw a man run down the stairs, jump into a big yellow car, and drive away. He couldn't give the make of the car. Somebody had been sprinkling tacks along Belton Drive. If you'll read the paper, you'll notice that a motorist saw this guy sweeping the tacks off the highway.

"There's a service station down on Belton Drive near Olive Street. About five minutes past nine Tuesday night, you drove in there. You had two flats, big tacks in each tire. The service station man jotted down the license number of your car.

"Okay, figure it out. You drove up to the house to meet Elaine Dixmer. There weren't any tacks on the road then. You drove back, and there were tacks on the road. Another guy comes along a few minutes later and sees a fellow sweeping the tacks off the road. What's the answer?"

Marr paused.

Gost picked up a pencil and started sliding it through his thumb and forefinger. "Go ahead," he said, without looking up. "You're doing swell."

"I'll tell you the answer," Marr said. "Those tacks were put there for you. That means you didn't commit the murder—not in the opinion of a jury, but in my opinion. And right now, my opinion is what counts.

"These guys knew you were going to be at the house. They knew Elaine Dixmer was there. They knew you had a motive for bumping her off. That probably means she was trying to blackmail you. They figured that if something happened, and you had a chance to get away, you'd take it on the lam. They wanted to be certain they could prove that you were in the neighborhood at the time. They did that by forcing you to stop at the service station.

"They didn't figure on the service station guy taking

down your license number. They didn't want the police to have any clues to work on, but they *did* want it so the service station man could identify you if he saw you again.

"All right, what does that add up to? Blackmail."

Gost said, "You're crazy as hell, but this is a new experience, and I like new experiences. I suppose you'll wind up trying to sell me life insurance."

"Exactly," Marr said. "Not the kind that pays your relatives dough after you kick off, but the kind that keeps you from getting gassed in a little room up in San Quentin."

Gost looked up at Marr, then lowered his eyes to the pencil which he kept sliding up and down in his fingers. "You're crazy," he said. "I suppose the only thing to do is to humor you."

Marr nodded.

"And just for the sake of humoring you," Gost said, "how do you figure more than one man was mixed up in it?"

Marr said, "That depends on when you drove up to the house. If you'd been there some time, one man could have done it. If you weren't there long, it took two men."

"How do you figure?"

"This neighbor heard a woman scream. He saw you come running out of the house. Okay, it took something to make that woman scream. Someone was there. Also someone had to put tacks on the highway. That was done after you drove up and before you drove back. I figure at least two men."

Gost said, "Just what do you propose to do, Mr. Marr?"

Marr said, "The way I figure it, it's blackmail. If they just wanted a fall guy for the killing, they'd have tipped off the police, and the police would have been at that service station before this. They're sitting tight. That means they figure the thing will blow over, and they'll be in a swell position to turn plenty of heat on you.

"They haven't approached the guy at the service station

yet. That means it's too hot for them to handle. They won't wait too long because they don't want him to forget what you look like. That service station is for sale. Twenty-five hundred bucks will swing the deal. We'd buy the service station and plant a ringer on the job."

"Then what?" Gost asked.

Jerry Marr grinned. "Then," he said, "you leave things entirely in my hands."

Gost nervously twisted the pencil back and forth in his fingers. At length he said, "I know you're crazy. You must think I'm crazy. Perhaps I am, but I'm not crazy enough to let my hair down to a man I've never seen before. Give me some references. I'll look you up, and tomorrow morning at this time we'll talk."

Jerry Marr laughed. The laugh was harsh, grating, and sarcastic. He said, "We won't wait until tomorrow morning. I'll give you references right now."

"Who?" Gost asked.

"You."

"Me?"

"Yes."

"What do you mean? What are you getting at?"

Marr said, "I've got the goods on you. I can pin a murder rap on you. I can go to the police and be the fair-haired boy child. I could bust into print and get a lot of publicity. I could come to you and tell you to shell across with five grand, or I'd tell the cops what I knew. I don't do that. I come to you and show you how you can get off the spot."

Gost's eyes hardened. "How do I know you're not going to try that anyway?"

"Because I'm not striking while the iron's hot."

"If I hire you, then you *will* have something on me."

Marr gave an exclamation of disgust. "Snap out of it, brother," he said. "This is certainly a hell of a time for *you* to be cautious."

Gost fidgeted uneasily in his chair for a moment, then he picked up the telephone and said to the girl at the switchboard, "Have Gertrude go down to the bank and get me twenty-five hundred dollars in cash."

"I'll need some for expenses," Marr reminded him.

"Make it three thousand," Gost said into the transmitter. "Have her make out a check payable to cash. Bring it in, and I'll sign it."

Jerry Marr heaved a slow sigh of contented relaxation. He got up and walked across to the window of the sumptuous office. Clouds were breaking away, and patches of clear, blue sky were showing above the tops of the downtown office buildings.

The big Cadillac with worn tires slid smoothly into the service station. Two men got to the ground. The one who squirmed out from behind the steering wheel was stocky, swarthy, and level-browed. The man who climbed from the other door was tall, slightly stooped, thin, and poker-faced. He had steady gray eyes that made a slow survey of the service station and finally came to rest on the freckle-faced youth who came forward with a friendly grin and said, "Fill 'er up, gents?"

"You run this place?" the tall man asked.

"I work here."

"Who runs it?"

"The guy who lives in the house."

"How long you been working here?"

"Just a day and a half."

"How about the man in the house?"

"He lives here. He runs the joint."

"Get him," the tall man said.

The freckled-faced youth scurried across to the front door of the house and knocked. A moment later Jerry Marr, a growth of stubble on his face, his broad shoulders held forward into a slouch which was emphasized by the sagging lines of a coat, stood blinking over steel-rimmed spectacles.

The tall man said, "You run the place?"

"Yes."

"We want to ask you a few questions."

"What about?"

"About Tuesday night."

"You mean this last Tuesday?"

"That's right."

"That was the night they had the murder up the street?"

"That's it."

"What about it?"

"You fixed some flats on a car that night."

Jerry Marr scratched his head, his fingers working through the tangled mass of thick, wavy, black hair. "Well now, let's see," he said. ". . . Tuesday night . . . flat . . ."

The shorter man interrupted him patiently. "A yellow car. Two flats with a—"

"Shut up, Pete," the tall man said in an even voice, without taking his eyes from Jerry Marr.

"The yellow car?" Jerry asked.

"*You* tell us about the car," the tall man said.

"But I don't remember no car."

"Weren't you here Tuesday?"

"That's right, yes."

"And Tuesday night a little after nine o'clock, didn't you change a couple of tires on a car?"

"Well, now," Jerry said, "seems to me I did. Come to think of it, I guess I did. That's right, a couple of flats, and they had some roofing tacks stuck plumb through the casing. That's right. I remember it now."

The men exchanged glances.

"What sort of a car was it?" the tall man asked.

"Gosh, I couldn't tell you that," Jerry said. "I just changed the tires, that's all. He was a nice chap though. He gave me two and a half. I remember now, it was sort of sprinkling, and he was in a hurry."

"Can't you remember what the car looked like?"

Marr said, "Well, now, wait a minute. I think it was a roadster or a coupé. I don't think it was a touring car."

"What color was it?"

Marr screwed his face into a perplexed frown. "Well, now," he began slowly.

"Wait a minute," the tall man interrupted. "Here. Take a look at this picture, and see if you recognize it."

Jerry Marr took the picture of Frank Gost which the tall man handed him. He adjusted steel-rimmed spectacles on the bridge of his nose, peered owlishly through them, and slowly shook his head. "What is he," he asked, "a politician or something?"

"He's the guy who drove the car," the stocky man said.

"Which car?"

"The one we're talking about, the one that had the flat tires."

"Oh, yes. The flat tires," Jerry said. "Why, sure."

"Say, what's the matter with you?" the tall man asked.

"With me?"

"Yes."

"Nothing." Marr shook his head.

"Haven't you any memory at all?"

"Well, I don't know as it's so good as some people's," Jerry said, "but I get along all right with it. We have lots of people come here, mister. I can't remember every one of them. If they don't pay for what they take, I try to remember long enough to see that it gets written down, but sometimes if another customer drives up before I get into the cash register, I skip it completely.

"Lots of times people will come in here and start shelling out money and tell me they owe it to me, and to save my life I can't remember nothin' about it."

The tall man said, "All right. Never mind that. You'd recognize this chap who was driving the yellow car, wouldn't you?"

"What yellow car?"

"The one with the two flats."

Jerry frowned. "I didn't say it was yellow," he said.

"Well, it was yellow. We know it was yellow. It was a yellow convertible, a—"

"I don't think it was yellow," Jerry said obstinately.

The tall man showed impatience. "Listen," he said, "do you know what happens to guys who try to dumb-up on the cops?"

"Are you a cop?" Jerry asked.

"We're investigating that murder," the tall man said.

"Oh."

"And you know what happens to guys who try to cover up?"

"I don't know what you mean."

"Why try to give the cops the runaround?"

"I don't want to give you no runaround," Jerry said. "I'm trying to tell you."

The tall man's eyes glittered frostily. "Okay," he said. "I'm going to look you up. If you're on the square, you'll remember this man in the yellow car. If you're trying to cover up, it's going to be just too bad for you. If you've taken any dough, you'll get nailed as an accessory to a murder. Now, let that soak in."

Jerry's face maintained its urbane, simple smile. "I don't know what you're talkin' about, gents," he said. "You asked me about that car, and I'm trying to think of it. I remember the car with the two flats all right, and I think it was a coupé, but I don't think it was yellow. I think it was a dark red. You know, just about the shade that—"

The short-coupled, swarthy man muttered an epithet and moved forward.

The tall man restrained him. "If you could see this man a couple of times," he said, "you'd remember him, wouldn't you?"

"I might."

"This picture doesn't look like him?"

"Well, I'll tell you, mister. I was never much of a hand to look at pictures and place people. In fact, I don't go so good on remembering faces. But, shucks, I could remember a man from Tuesday night. Sure, I could tell if I saw him again."

"Okay," the tall man said. "We'll be back later, and in the meantime, don't you talk to anyone. You get me? Don't talk to anyone about our being here. This is police business, and it's very confidential."

Jerry said, with that disarming grin of stupid simplicity, "Shucks, now, boys. I know enough not to do that. Why, I could forget all about you having been here inside of two minutes after you left."

The tall man turned to the one whom he had addressed as Pete. "Hell," he said, "he could at that."

"Now you just go right ahead chasing down your clues," Jerry said, "and if I can help you, all you've got to do is say so."

"We're going to spot you where you can see this man," the tall one said. "We aren't going to make any mistakes. We'll point out the man who was driving that car. If you don't identify him, it's going to be just too bad for you. Do you get that? Just too bad for you."

"Oh, sure," Jerry said. "I'll identify him if he's the right one. But I was selling a lot of gas that night and doing a lot of chores around the station."

The tall man turned to Pete. "Let's go," he said.

The freckle-faced kid twisted his fingers around the gas cap of the Cadillac automobile. "Want some gas?" he asked.

"Naw," Pete said, sliding in behind the steering wheel of the car and slamming the door shut with a vicious jerk.

Jerry Marr stepped back in the little house. He jerked off the steel-rimmed glasses, whipped off the coat, put on his own double-breasted coat, pulled a felt hat down low on his forehead, dashed out of the back door, and gunned the motor of his flivver into life.

As the big Cadillac slid smoothly down the block, Marr's car bounced across the curb and took up the trail.

The Cadillac pulled rapidly ahead. Marr kept his car behind, desiring above all things not to arouse suspicion in the minds of his quarry.

For more than two miles Marr trailed along behind. Then he started giving his car more speed, closing the gap between the two machines. Traffic was thicker here, and it was a good opportunity for Marr to jockey his car into a more favorable position.

Suddenly the Cadillac veered to the left, crossed at a signal intersection ahead of the oncoming traffic, and vanished.

Jerry Marr promptly pulled his own car to the left, ran for two blocks, and then turned right on a street paralleling the boulevard. When he came to the cross street down which the Cadillac had turned, there was no sign of the car anywhere in sight. Marr cruised up and down the street, making a note of the houses, hoping to find the Cadillac parked in a driveway.

At the end of a fruitless ten minutes, Marr turned back to the boulevard and returned to the service station.

LORRAIN DELL sat across the nightclub table from Jerry Marr and sipped a liqueur. "All right," she said. "Let's have it."

"Have what?" Marr asked.

"Knowing you as I do," she said, "I realize that when a young woman receives an invitation to dine with you, is plied with liquor, gorged with food, and flattered with attention, you have some ulterior motive in mind."

"Have you taken into consideration the well-known biological urge?"

"Yes," she said, "and rejected it."

He arched his eyebrows in a gesture of interrogation.

"You started out to be a lawyer," she said. "The depression licked you. You tried to get a job and couldn't. You started in as a special investigator. You didn't get any business. You decided to go after business. To quote your own words, 'no damned depression is going to lick me.' You are now engaged in battling the depression singlehanded. You are far too busy and far too intent on winning to even notice biological urges, let alone surrender to them."

Jerry Marr grinned. "Your grounds for the accusation?" he asked.

"For one thing, you haven't even noticed my dress."

Jerry surveyed the curve of the shoulders visible above the bodice of the evening gown.

"Nice," he said.

"Isn't it? I suppose you noticed it as soon as you saw me."

"Indeed I did," Marr said. "It's—"

"What color is the sash?" she asked.

"Blue," Marr said promptly.

Lorrain Dell shook her head sadly. "You're absolutely hopeless," she said. "Come on, Jerry. Get it off your chest. To what do I owe this sudden excess of interest?"

Jerry said, "I thought you might like to pick up a little extra money."

"Now we're getting somewhere. Doing what?"

"A little detective work."

"You look here, Jerry. You know I can't. Mother would die if she thought I was getting mixed up in anything like that. I told you that before. There are lots of good-looking girls who can do anything I can and a lot more besides who are crazy for the business, women who are regular operatives and—"

"But I can't hire them," Jerry said.

"Why?"

"Because I can't trust them."

"Can't you trust them to dig out facts—do what you call the leg work?"

"Of course," Jerry said. "But I can't tell what they'll do with it after they get it. This is something big. The least slip might spoil it. Anyone who smelled a rat, found out what I was working on, and tried to cut in on a bit of the gravy would put me in an awful spot."

"Why, Jerry?"

"I'm working on something big for someone big. If I

do this thing the way it should be done, I can count on an influential friend and a lot of business to follow. If I don't do it the way it should be done, I'll be all washed up."

"What do you want me to do?" she asked.

Marr said, "That's better. Here's a paper label. You can see where a cost mark and a selling price were written in pencil. It's pretty dim now, but I've photographed the label in a side lighting which brings out the shadows."

Jerry showed her the original label and the photographic copy. On the photographic copy the figures showing the cost code and the sale price were plainly visible.

"What about it?" she asked.

Jerry said, "Go to the hardware jobbers. See if you can get a clue as to the store that has that cost mark. Go to the store and see if they remember making a sale to a tall, sandy-haired chap with stoop shoulders, gray eyes, and a thin mouth, or to a chunky man in the middle thirties with a swarthy complexion and eyebrows that almost join in the bridge of his nose."

"And then?" she asked.

"Then," Marr said, "use the greatest discretion. Find out if the hardware store knows these people, where they live, whether they're regular customers—and watch your step because it's dangerous."

"Do you have any leads at all?" she asked.

"Not to amount to anything," Jerry said. "They drive a late Cadillac. The car is registered to a man by the name of Dikes in San Francisco. He's moved away. No one knows where he is. There's no change of address on file with the Motor Vehicle Department. I *think* the pair have a hangout around West Seventy-fifth Street. I trailed them that far and lost them. They may have got wise. They may have turned into a hideout. I don't know."

"Why don't you do it yourself, Jerry?"

"It would make too much comment for one thing. For another, I have to stick around the service station I've bought."

"You've bought a service station?"

"Yes."

"Good heavens, why?"

He grinned. "So a couple of chaps can get rough with me."

"These same two?"

"Yes."

"How rough will they get, Jerry?"

"I don't know," he said, and then after a moment added, "How rough would you get to change a one-way ticket to the death cell into a million-dollar blackmail?"

"Plenty," she said.

Marr nodded.

She studied him for a few thoughtful seconds, her eyes, hazel and steady, showing a willingness to cope with the world as she found it, her head and shoulders carried in a manner which spoke of jaunty independence, her hands showing the effect of the roughest sort of housework.

Five years before, she and her mother had been independently wealthy. Now they lived in a little tumbledown bungalow. Her mother took in dressmaking, and Lorrain went to night school four nights a week, studying shorthand and typing. Daytimes she helped her mother with the sewing and did all the housework and cooking.

"How long do you think it will take, Jerry?" she asked.

"Perhaps two days. Perhaps two months. You'll need a car. You'll have to hire someone to come in and do the work. You'll be paid twelve dollars a day and expenses. You'll have to pretend you're a bill collector or in charge of credit at a lumber company. You'll have to make it stick by turning on enough personality to dazzle the men you're talking with into a state of hypnotic quiescence."

"Should I," she asked demurely, "start practicing on you?"

"Use me as sort of a punching bag?" Jerry asked.

"Kind of a guinea pig," she said, flashing him a dazzling smile.

Jerry Marr pushed his liqueur glass to one side, hooked his finger over the edge of an ashtray, and said, "If you think that makes me quiescent, you're crazy as hell."

The big yellow convertible turned into the service station and came to a stop by the gasoline pump.

Marr, his steel-rimmed glasses down low on his nose, came ambling forward, stoop-shouldered and awkward. "Evening, folks," he said.

The girl who was with Frank W. Gost looked at Marr curiously. Gost frowned darkly. He seemed to be in something of a temper.

Marr wiped off the windshield, looked up and down the highway, and then said, "Get my telephone message?"

"Yes," Gost said. "You've got a hell of a crust wanting money now."

Marr looked across at the young woman, a platinum-haired, sable-coated young woman with dancing eyes and red lips. He said to Gost, "Come in. I want to talk with you. . . . Why don't you get rid of that car?"

"It's too late now," Gost said. "They know who I am."

Marr said, "They knew who *you* were all the time."

"Well," Gost asked irritably, "what are you doing about it?"

Marr said, "I don't know yet. Come in here. I want to talk with you."

Gost said, "Excuse me," to the girl and followed Marr into the house.

Marr took off his steel-rimmed spectacles, slipped out of his coat, and straightened the slump out of his shoulders. "Bring that money?" he asked.

"You've had enough money."

"That's what you think. Did you bring it?"

"I'm not going to pay it over unless you can show me some results."

"What's happened to you?"

"They've called on me."

"Who has?"

"A short, chunky guy who looks something like an Italian."

"What did he want?"

"Wanted twenty-five thousand dollars," he said. "Otherwise they were going to tip the police off."

"They haven't any evidence," Marr said. "Tell them to go to hell."

Gost seemed uneasy.

"Well," Marr asked, "what's the matter?"

"There are some things about this you don't know about."

"Naturally," Marr said. "I'm playing it blind."

Gost took a cigar from his pocket, clipped off the end, and whipped a match into flame on the sole of his shoe. "What do you want more money for?"

"Expenses," Marr said.

"What expenses?"

"For one thing, a girl who's chasing down the hardware-store angle. I want to find out where those tacks came from."

"That's like looking for a needle in a haystack," Gost objected.

"I don't think so," Marr said.

"And what's more, I thought it was understood you were going to play a lone hand in this."

"She's all right," Marr said. "I'll vouch for her."

Gost flared into temper. "You haven't done anything that I can see. They've moved in on me and want money, and later on they'll be wanting more money."

"You didn't give it to them, did you?" Marr asked.

"I told him I'd give it to him tomorrow night."

"Tomorrow night?"

"Yes. You've got until then."

"You should have told him to go to hell."

"Yes, I should," Gost said. "The way *you're* working I'd be in jail by this time."

"Forget it," Marr said. "They aren't going to go to the police."

"That's what you say."

"Of course it's what I say. There's no money in it for them if they went to the police. If someone offers a reward, that'll be different."

Gost laughed nervously and said, "Well, there's no reward. No one puts up money for a tart like that."

"She's dead," Marr pointed out.

"She got what was coming to her," Gost said.

Marr said doggedly, "I want some money. I want to know the whole background."

Gost took out his wallet. He counted out five hundred dollars. "That's every cent I'm going to give you," he said, "and I'm not going to tell you a damn thing."

Marr didn't pick up the money. "I need a thousand," he said.

"You're getting five hundred."

The telephone rang. Marr cupped the receiver to his ear and heard Lorrain Dell's mother say, "Jerry, I'm frightfully worried about Lorrain. You don't know what she's doing, do you?"

"A little research work, I understand," Jerry said glibly. "What about her?"

"She hasn't come home yet."

"When did she go out?"

"Right after lunch."

"When did she expect to return?"

"At six o'clock, for dinner."

"Well," Marr said, "it's only eight-thirty now. She was probably detained. . . . Tell you what I'll do. I'll take a run over. You don't know where she is, do you?"

"No. I don't even know what she's working on. It's something she keeps looking up in the telephone book."

"I'll be over," Jerry promised.

He hung up the telephone and turned to Marr. "That girl who was working for me has disappeared."

"Well," Gost said irritably, "I can't help that."

Marr stared at him for a moment with his lips tightening into a thin, straight line. Abruptly he reached out and grabbed Gost by the necktie. "The hell you can't," he said, pushing the astonished broker back against the wall. "You can help it, and you're going to help it. There's more than your skin involved in this thing. You're holding out something on me, and I want it."

"There's five hundred dollars," Gost said. "Take it and get to work. Get your hands off me."

Marr tightened his grip. "All right," he said grimly, "if it takes blackmail to make you listen to reason, I'll try a little blackmail. You come through and come through right now, or I blow the lid off."

"What do you mean?"

Marr said, "There's the telephone. I call Police Headquarters and tell them the whole story."

Gost's face blanched. He raised his hands, wrapped the fingers around Marr's wrist, and said, "You wouldn't dare do that. Take you hands off me."

"Why wouldn't I dare to do it?" Marr asked, twisting the necktie a trifle.

"Because it would put you in the same boat with me."

"To hell with that," Marr said. "It would give that girl a break. The police could find her in an hour. The investigation that it's taking us days to work on they could get as a matter of routine."

Gost said, "You can't crowd me, Marr. I've warned you . . ."

"Oh, hell!" Marr said in disgust, throwing Gost back against the wall. "I should have known better than to waste time with a four-flusher anyway."

He walked to the telephone, dialed *Operator,* and said, "Connect me with Police Headquarters. Hurry."

Gost stared at him for a second in wide-eyed apprehension, then he came across the room to grab Marr's shoulder. "No, no," he said. "Don't. You can't. It would ruin me. They've got me. I can't get out of it."

Marr slowly dropped the receiver back into its cradle. "Go ahead," he said. "Start talking."

"I tell you I can't stand it," Gost said. "I'm in too deep. They have too much on me. I—"

Marr grabbed him by the coat, shook him, said, "To hell with that stuff. What I want is the lowdown. Give it to me quick."

"What do you want?"

"All about Elaine Dixmer. All about the murder."

Gost said, "She was blackmailing me. It started out easy and kept getting worse. I gave in to her, and that just whetted her appetite. I wrote her that girls got killed for things like that. Tuesday I went to see her. I heard her scream just as I got near the house. I got in and tried her bedroom door. It was locked. I could hear struggling, then someone jumped out a window. I had to go out to the window to get in. She was lying on the floor, strangled. A neighbor was yelling for the police. I beat it. I couldn't afford to be found then."

"You wrote her a threatening letter?" Marr asked.

"Yes. I'd been drinking, and she'd been crowding me. I was furious."

"Where's that letter now?" Marr asked.

"They have it," Gost said.

Marr stared moodily at the telephone, his face a mask of frowning concentration.

"What was she to you?" he asked.

"What do you think?"

"Did you love her?"

"Hell, no!"

"Who's the girl in the car?"

"She's going to marry me next month."

"Does she know about Elaine Dixmer?"

"No."

Marr said, "Tell her."

"I can't," Gost said. "She wouldn't understand. She's emotional, hot-blooded, and insanely jealous. She doesn't understand. You see, we—we've been going together, and the marriage has been arranged for . . ."

"Go out and tell her," Marr said, "or do you want me to?"

Gost avoided Marr's eyes.

"Give me five hundred dollars more," Marr said. "Get out and tell her, then come to this address."

He scribbled Lorrain Dell's address on a little sheet of notepaper.

Gost opened his wallet, counted out five one-hundred-dollar bills, and added them to the bills on the cash register.

Marr switched out the lights in the service station and said, "I'm going out and lock up those gas pumps. That'll give you your chance to tell her. Then meet me at that address—and don't be more than twenty minutes."

MRS. DELL came to the door in answer to Marr's ring. She was a woman who at fifty-five had retained the graceful lines of her figure. Her step was light and springy, but the battle with life had left lines on her face, and her eyes were tired and had lost their luster, like varnish which has been too long exposed to the weather.

Marr lost no time in formalities. "You don't know where she was going?" he asked.

"No."

"Do you know what she was doing?"

"No, I don't, Jerry. It was some sort of research work. She didn't want me to know about it, so I didn't inquire too closely. I know how you young people are."

"Was she working from a telephone book?" Jerry asked.

"I think she was."

"Have you looked in her room to see what you could find?"

"Yes. There are some notes, but I can't read them. They're written in shorthand—the names of some hardware companies that she's taken from the phone book."

Jerry said, "I wonder if you'd mind getting those things for me. I may be able to tell something from looking them over."

Mrs. Dell, without a word, turned and ran lightly up the stairs to Lorrain's bedroom. While she was gone, Frank Gost drove up, and Jerry, opening the door for him, was surprised to find that the girl in the expensive fur coat was with him.

"Miss Starling, may I present Mr. Marr?" Gost mumbled.

She gave Marr her hand. Her long, slender fingers gripped his hand with cool competence. She said, "Thank you for making him tell me, Mr. Marr. I had known just enough to be more than curious—decidedly uneasy."

Mrs. Dell came back downstairs. Jerry introduced Miss Starling and Gost as friends of his. They took Lorrain's notes and went into the dining room while Mrs. Dell returned to the chair under the floor light in which she had been sitting, sewing. She peered out toward the dining room, then sighed, adjusted her glasses, and started once more plying her needle in swift, sure strokes, her thimble glittering in the light.

In the dining room Jerry said, "Now keep your voices low. I'm trying to find out where she went. Here's a list of hardware stores with shorthand after them. By any chance do you read shorthand, Miss Starling?"

"Yes," she said. "My folks wanted me to absorb the knowledge of the so-called idle rich, but my experience has been that the girls who are *really* independent are the hustling poor. So when my dad sent me to Paris to study art, I played hooky, went to a business college, and took a course. He'd die if he found it out."

"Can you read this?" Marr asked.

"I'm not so darned good at reading," she said. "Let's see. Here's Central Hardware Company, and after that there's something about . . . about . . . It looks like 'Cost mark uses same letters, but price not right on tacks.' Gosh, that's a wild guess."

Marr said, "I think that's right."

"Just what do you expect to gain by this, Marr?" Gost

asked. "She wouldn't be at a hardware store. She'd have gone to the people who bought the tacks."

Jerry shook his head. "Not Lorrain," he said. "She'd have followed instructions. Here's what must have happened. These people must either own a hardware store or have a relative who clerks in a hardware store. Lorrain made inquiries of the wrong persons. They decided to take steps to see that the information didn't reach me."

"You think she's been silenced?"

"At least temporarily," Jerry said.

Vivian Starling said, "These others are all just about the same. Those shorthand notes all amount to the same thing. One of them reads 'Wrong price for tacks.' Another one—"

"I've got it," Jerry interrupted. "This is the list of hardware stores in the vicinity of Seventy-fifth Street. She's taken them from the telephone book. The ones with the shorthand after them are the ones she's covered. This list is a carbon copy, so she must have the original with her. . . . Oh, Mrs. Dell."

Mrs. Dell dropped her sewing and looked up, squinting her eyes against the brilliant illumination of the floor lamp as she tried to see into the dining room. "Yes?" she asked.

"Did Lorrain do any writing when she was home for lunch? Did she make any notes, do you know?"

"No, she didn't—that is, I don't think she did."

Marr said, "Thanks," to Mrs. Dell, and then said in a low voice to Gost, "All right, she makes them at night. This is her second day on the case. She covered fifteen stores the first day. Let's figure that she got six stores this morning. It takes her a little time to win the confidence of the manager, you know, and she may have gone faster or slower. But let's start in with this seventh store and make inquiries."

"What sort of inquiries?" Gost asked.

Marr said, "Go to the drugstores or restaurants nearby that are open. Find out if the people know the ones who own the hardware stores. Get descriptions of the proprietors or the clerks. Say you're looking for a relative who lives there."

Jerry folded the paper along the line of the shorthand writing. He slit the paper in two, then with his knife again divided it. "You take the seventh, eighth, ninth, and tenth, Gost," he said. "I'll take the eleventh, twelfth, thirteenth, fourteenth, and fifteenth. We'd better report by telephone every half hour. How can we do it?"

Vivian Starling said, "I'll give you my number. My butler is one of those well-trained instruments of human perfection. If you find anything, telephone him that Miss Starling has asked you to say that she will meet Mr. Gost at whatever address you have in mind. If we find anything, I'll telephone him that if Mr. Marr calls up and asks for a message, he's to meet me at a certain place. No messages mean no progress."

Marr clapped on his hat, pushed the list down in his pocket, and started for the door. "I think she's being detained on some work in a library where they don't allow patrons to use the telephone and where they can't leave a pile of reference papers once they've taken it out," he said glibly but vaguely to Mrs. Dell. "I'll take a run down there."

"I can't see why she wouldn't have telephoned," Mrs. Dell said, worry in her voice.

Marr patted her shoulder. "That's all right," he said. "I'm satisfied that's what it is. I think this is an important job she's on, getting some information for a bunch of hardware jobbers."

They left the house, Gost and Vivian Starling entering the long-nosed, expensive convertible with its white-walled tires and glistening chrome. But it was Marr's battered flivver which rattled away first and which led by a good fifty yards at the boulevard intersection.

Following a hunch, Jerry started with the last of his list first. The hardware store that he wanted was dark, as was to have been expected, but a drugstore on the corner was open. Jerry made discreet inquiries and found that the proprietor was a thin, short, bald-headed man in his sixties.

He looked at his watch when he had finished gathering the information. It was exactly twenty minutes since he had left Lorrain's house. The next hardware store on his list was also dark. Jerry drove two blocks before he found a little restaurant which was just closing up for the night. The proprietor, an old German, knew the men who ran the hardware store. He nodded his head in response to Jerry's question. "Two men," he said, "partners. One of them is tall and bald with gray eyes and a couple of gold teeth. That's Oscar Tollman. The other is short with big, black eyebrows. He's dark. His name is Brogler. I've heard the first name, but I don't remember. I—"

"Pete Brogler?" Marr interrupted.

"That's it," the German beamed. "That's it. I remember now. It's Pete."

Marr pushed him to one side as he raced back to the telephone. He pawed through the pages and found a residence address of Oscar Tollman. There was nothing under the name of Brogler.

Marr dropped in a nickel, dialed the number Vivian Starling had given him, and when he heard the painfully correct voice of the butler on the line, said, "Mr. Marr talking. Has Miss Starling left any message for me?"

"No, Mr. Marr. Could I take a message for her?"

"Yes." Jerry said. "If Mr. Gost calls, tell him that Miss Starling said she would meet him at the residence of Oscar Tollman, that Tollman was the man he wanted. Do you have that straight?"

"Of course, sir. The man Mr. Gost wanted."

"That's right," Marr said.

"And the address, sir?"

Marr gave it to him.

"Very good, sir."

Marr raced from the store while the fat German proprietor stood looking at him with puckered brows and dubious eyes.

Marr pushed his flivver into speed, parked it half a block from Tollman's house, and walked rapidly down the sidewalk. There were no lights in the house.

Marr passed the house, turned into an adjoining yard, working through to the backyard, and started back toward the place he wanted. A nervous terrier from one of the houses kept up an incessant, high-pitched hysterical barking. Marr could hear the gruff voice of a man telling the dog to be still, that there was nothing to bark at, then Marr climbed the fence and dropped into the yard he wanted. The back of the house, he saw, also was dark.

Jerry had no time to waste with such formalities as ringing doorbells. A small pocket flashlight, hardly larger than a fountain pen, showed him there was a key in the lock of the back door. Jerry was preparing to punch it out and insert a skeleton key when he thought to try the knob.

To his surprise the door was unlocked.

Jerry stepped into the kitchen. The room seemed warm. There was the smell of cigarette smoke in the air.

Jerry switched out the flashlight, eased his gun from its shoulder holster, and tiptoed forward into the darkness. In the middle of the room he once more tried a brief flash of light which gave him the direction of a swinging door, apparently leading to a serving pantry. Jerry didn't use his flashlight again, but slipped noiselessly through the swinging door, crossed the serving pantry, found another swinging door which led from the serving pantry to the dining room. He gently opened this door and stood in the velvety darkness listening.

He was conscious of a peculiar sensation on his right cheek. For a moment he couldn't place it. Then he realized it was a subtle emanation of warmth as though someone were standing close to him.

Jerry swung the gun and prodded sharply to the side.

The gun muzzle encountered nothing, yet the warmth was still on his cheek.

He dared not risk a beam from the flashlight, but, holding it in his left hand, he felt out with his fingertips toward the source of that warmth. His right hand held the gun ready for instant action.

His left hand did not have far to go, only a matter of inches, and then there was the tinkling sound of metal against glass as the flashlight rubbed gently against the hot sides of a lighting fixture.

Jerry stood perfectly still as the significance of that warm light fixture penetrated to his consciousness.

They had known in some way that he was coming. They had waited for him. The house was a trap. The back door had been left unlocked—probably the front door as well. But how had they known he had located them and was on his way?

Jerry thought back to the German restaurant keeper. There had been a look of suspicion on his face as Jerry had dashed out of the door. Jerry had been too eager, too excited, and in too much of a hurry. The German had undoubtedly gone to the telephone and notified Tollman. Tollman had switched out the lights and . . .

Jerry thought he could hear the faint rustle of motion from a corner of the dining room as someone moved.

Jerry's whole school of fighting had been that a swift offensive is worth a dozen defensive campaigns. He swung his flashlight in the direction of the motion, held the gun just above the flashlight, and pushed the button.

The small globe of the flashlight sent a beam toward the far end of the room. Jerry was conscious of someone standing there, a tall, stooped figure.

"Stick 'em up," Jerry said, and his finger tightened on the trigger.

To his complete surprise the figure raised its arms, holding its hands extended palms outward.

"What are you doing in my house?" a voice asked.

And it was just as Jerry started to answer the question

that he became conscious of a slight pressure in his back, a pressure which suddenly increased to a firm push, and an ominous voice said, "This is a sawed-off shotgun, brother."

For an instant Jerry hesitated.

From behind him came the swishing sound of motion. A blackjack thudded down on Jerry's right shoulder.

Volition left Jerry's arm. It dropped down to his side. The nerveless fingers relaxed, and the gun thudded to the floor. The figure at the far end of the room clicked a light switch, and Jerry found himself facing the expressionless gray eyes of Oscar Tollman.

From behind, Pete Brogler gave him a shove which sent him staggering into the room. Brogler picked up Jerry's gun from the floor, shoved it in his pocket, said, "Sit down and tell us about it," and gestured toward a chair with the muzzle of his gun.

Tollman said, "Wait a minute, Pete. First the girl. Now this guy. Perhaps Gost comes next."

"Nuts," Brogler said. "Gost hasn't got guts enough."

Tollman said, "I don't like it. Let's get out long enough to take stock of the situation."

Marr, holding his numbed right arm with his left hand, trying to massage some life into it, said, "You aren't dealing with Gost. You're dealing with the police."

Tollman laughed sardonically.

Brogler said, "Okay, Oscar. That covers it. If anyone else was coming, he wouldn't try to make us think the police were going to crash in on the party."

"You can't tell about him," Tollman said. "He's smart enough to have figured that out. You know damn well if he'd said no one else was wise, we'd whisk him out of here figuring Gost was on his way out, and he knows that if he had told us Gost was on his way out, we'd figure it as a play to make us stick around. So he pulls this police business. Go ahead and frisk him."

Tollman slipped his gun from a shoulder holster. Brogler said carelessly, "Aw, he's clean. These birds only carry one rod—and don't know how to use that. I tell you it's okay. Dutch only mentioned one guy."

Tollman reached his decision. "I don't give a damn what Dutch said, and I don't care what you say. We're on our way. Frisk him, and let's get started.'

Brogler grabbed the shoulder of Marr's coat, jerked him to his feet, ran an expert hand over Marr's clothes, and said, "Yeah, he's clean. Just the one rod."

Tollman said, "Let's go."

Marr dropped back into the chair. "Let's talk this thing over, boys," he said.

"What do you have to offer?" Brogler wanted to know.

"Cut me in," Marr said, "and I'll show you how to make a real cleanup."

Tollman said, "Wait a minute, Pete. We've seen this lad before somewhere."

Pete frowned. "That's what I was thinking."

Suddenly Tollman gave an exclamation. "The service station," he said. "Put a pair of steel-rimmed spectacles on that guy's nose, slouch his shoulders forward, just a little powder in his hair, and—"

"By heaven, you're right," Brogler said.

Marr said easily, "I was trying to cut myself in on the deal. Naturally, I wanted all of it for me. It's too big. There's too much of it. I had you guys figured early in the game. I decided to contact you and put up a proposition."

Brogler said, "What's the proposition?"

"A three-way split," Marr said, "and we pool information."

Tollman said, "Don't let him fool you, Pete. He's sparring for time. He's trying to hold us here. I tell you, someone else *is* coming."

Brogler knitted his heavy brows in thought, said, "I guess you're right at that. Okay, let's get him out."

Marr played his last card. "You can't shoot me here," he said, "and I'm not leaving."

He crossed his knees and settled back in the chair.

Tollman said, "We don't have to shoot you." He took a piece of light cord from his pocket, deftly knotted a bowline knot, and made a running noose.

"Same cord that was used on Elaine Dixmer," said Marr.

"My, aren't you bright," Tollman jeered. He tossed the cord to Brogler. Brogler twisted a free end around his thick fingers and approached Marr. "Coming?" he asked.

Marr pushed his head hard against the back of the chair. "I'm comfortable," he said. "I want to talk."

Brogler rushed. Tollman, holding a gun, moved ominously closer.

Marr doubled sharply forward from the waist, gripped the arms of the chair, and lunged. His head struck Brogler in the pit of the stomach with the force of a battering ram. Brogler staggered backward. Marr instinctively sidestepped, then swiftly whirled, and came up to face Tollman. He was close enough to slap the gun arm to one side, then send a right crashing to Tollman's jaw. Tollman staggered back but didn't let go of the gun. Marr lunged for it. He heard staggering steps behind him. Tollman tried to raise and point the gun. Marr grabbed for the gun arm, and Pete Brogler, staggering up from behind, flung his arms around Jerry's waist and clamped his legs around Jerry's. Before Jerry could shake him loose, Brogler had thrown him off balance. The two crashed heavily to the floor. Marr looked up to see the barrel of Tollman's gun describing a whirling arc. He tried to swing his head to one side. Brogler was holding him as in a vise.

The first blow didn't knock Jerry out. He experienced a brief wave of blackness and nausea, but he was conscious. He relaxed his muscles, groaned, closed his eyes, and waited, figuring that by feigning unconsciousness he could lure them into such a position that he would stand a fighting chance.

Brogler said, "Make a good job of it. I don't trust this guy."

Lying there with his eyes closed, thinking of his chances,

listening for the sound of Gost's motor, wondering what had happened to Lorrain and if she was in the house, Jerry was entirely unprepared for that which followed.

The gun butt crashed down on his head as though it had been a sledgehammer.

Jerry felt a great surge of darkness suck him down into the vast maw of night.

MARR was conscious of a sidewalk which swayed and pitched like the deck of a ship in a storm. He knew there were hands on each side holding him up. A voice was in his ear. "Walk. That's your service station. Go on in, you fool. You're home."

Marr saw the familiar outlines of the service station, outlines which were as unreal and distorted as a reflection seen in a convex mirror.

"Come on. Climb up those stairs. Shake a leg. We haven't got all night," the voices said. "Don't you want to go home?"

Jerry's legs were numb things which held no strength. His mind was engulfed in a blinding headache. His response to the voices was mechanical. He staggered up the steps. Someone flung open a door. He was pushed toward a couch. He tried to put out his hands to steady himself and then found that his hands were tied behind his back. His wobbling legs gave way under him, and he pitched forward to crash a shoulder against the couch.

The floor rose up and hit him a jarring smash on the side of the head, and for several long minutes he lay perfectly still.

Again he heard voices. He knew that Lorrain was in the room. . . . A toe prodded against his ribs. The voice of Brogler said, "All right, wise guy. Do you want to listen?"

Tollman said, "Let him alone. Don't gloat. Where's that dynamite?"

Marr struggled to get to a sitting position. His eyes took in Lorrain's white face. They were tying her up. It wasn't with rope. It was— Good heavens, it was with blasting fuse!

He stared incredulously and saw Tollman jerk her head back, place two brownish-yellow cylinders down inside of her blouse, pushing them down—down . . .

Marr knew the answer then. They were going to burn the place. Naturally there would be explosions. The police couldn't tell the difference between the explosion of dynamite and that of gasoline. There wouldn't be any sign of ropes around the bodies because the fuse would burn.

Marr said, somewhat thickly, "If anything happens to me, there's a letter left where it'll be delivered to the police."

"Old stuff," Tollman said. "Try something more original."

"It happens to be the truth," Marr said, and his voice sounded strange even to his own ears, as though it had been coming from a distant part of the room.

Tollman said, "Get going, Pete. Sling that gasoline hose in through the window."

"It won't reach that far," Brogler said.

"Tie another hose on the end of it. Splice it with a piece of water hose. Get the stuff in here."

Marr knew what he had to do. It was a desperate chance. He lurched to his knees. He could hold up his weight, but he didn't let them know that. He collapsed back to the floor, taking care to fall in such a position that his knees were in under him.

"Hurry up with that gas hose," Tollman said.

Brogler went out the back way. Tollman walked over to a window.

Marr raised himself to his knees. Getting to his feet was harder. It took grim concentration.

Over in the corner where Brogler had left her, Lorrain watched him with wide eyes.

Marr made it to his feet. There was a little desk over near the south window. In the drawer of that desk . . .

He stepped quickly to the window. Tollman heard the motion and whirled.

There was no time for finesse now. Marr shoved his shoulder against the window—hard. He felt the pane of glass give, then crash into tinkling fragments. He shoved his wrists half through the window and chopped down.

He felt a sharp edge of broken glass cutting his flesh. He knew Tollman was coming toward him. He spread his wrists and shoved down hard against the jagged edge of glass. The cords parted.

Tollman lunged.

Marr's groping hand caught the knob in the desk drawer, jerked it open. His left hand pushed Tollman off. Tollman was tugging at his hip pocket. His face twisted into a snarling mask.

Marr's hand closed on the butt of the gun.

Marr didn't hesitate. His motions were calm, deliberate in their finality, although fast as lightning in speed.

From outside the window Brogler called, "What the hell's the matter?"

The gun was an automatic. Marr felt the bouncing jar in his wrist as the recoil operated the reloading mechanism.

He fired twice.

Both bullets caught Tollman in the stomach. The first one blasted him back, brought a look of dazed, incredulous surprise to his poker face. The second one wiped all expression, all animation from his countenance.

Out in the graveled space by the gasoline pump, Brogler dropped a piece of water hose he had been coupling to the muzzle of one of the big gasoline hoses. His right hand streaked for his gun, got it from his pocket.

Brogler fired once. The bullet crashed through glass within an inch of Marr's head.

Marr fired three times.

Jerry ran to Lorrain Dell. He pushed his hand down the front of her blouse, felt the ends of the two round sticks of dynamite nestled against the smooth, rounded flesh. He pulled out the deadly cylinders and rolled them under the couch. It was hard to cut the fuse which had been wrapped around her. He unwrapped it and then cut the cords around her wrists.

Sirens were screaming by the time she had helped him push the powder fuse under the couch. A moment later a police car screamed to a stop at the curb.

Marr adjusted steel-rimmed spectacles, put on the coat which was too big for him across the shoulders, picked up the automatic, and went out.

"A stickup," he said, "but I got my gun."

"You're running this service station?"

"Yes."

"What happened?"

"Just a stickup. They pulled in and said they wanted my dough."

The officer seemed skeptical. "This," he said, "doesn't look like a stickup to me. It—"

He broke off as Frank Gost's big yellow convertible skidded around the corner in a screaming turn and then slid to a stop in front of the service station.

Gost flung open the door, started to get out, then saw the police car and stopped. The second officer, moving grimly forward, said, "Okay, buddy. Come on out. What was *your* hurry?"

Gost said, "I—er—"

Vivian Starling opened the door on the other side of the car. The officers had a flash of shapely legs, smiling lips, and white teeth. She came forward with easy assurance. "We were," she said, "looking for the police."

The officer who had been interrogating Jerry called out to his partner, "Don't overlook any bets. They claim this is a stickup, but it looks fishy to me. Look at the gasoline hose . . ."

"I can explain that," Marr interrupted quickly. "I wanted to put some gasoline in the air pump. I figured I could run the hose back—and then they drove up and got out. I thought they wanted some gas or road information. One of them batted me over the head and . . ."

"And," Vivian Starling said calmly, "that's where we came along. We saw the stickup. My boyfriend stepped on the gas, hoping we'd find an officer down at the intersection. No one was there, so I persuaded him to come back. The way they hit this man, I thought it might be a murder."

Gost said hurriedly, "Here's my card, Officer. If you need any witnesses . . ."

"No. It's all right," the officer said, and then to Marr, "You'd better go to the hospital with that head."

Marr said doggedly, "I stay right here."

One of the officers bent over Brogler. "Hey," he said. "This guy's conscious."

Marr observed almost casually, "The other guy's in bad shape. He knows he's going to die. He said this bird killed that woman up the street Tuesday night, stuck a piece of cord around her neck, and pulled it tight."

Brogler, lying flat, little sputtering bubbles of red froth on his lips, was still conscious enough to think fast. "He can't pin that on me," he said weakly.

One of the officers from the inside of the house said, "That guy croaked."

Brogler heaved a long, bubbling sigh. "He did it," he said. "She was two-timing him, and he slipped the cord around her neck. I didn't know anything about it until afterward."

"Who's the girl?" the officer asked Marr.

"My girl friend. She'd been out at the library doing some research work for the hardware jobbers, getting some information—statistics of some sort. I was going to take her home. She dropped in here. I was going to telephone her mother and say we were on our way out."

The officer asked Lorrain, "You saw this stickup?"

She nodded.

"It frightened her half to death," Marr explained.

One of the officers telephoned Headquarters. His voice

was jubilant. "A couple of stickups," he said. "One of them's dead. The other will last a couple of hours, and that's all. It clears up that Dixmer murder Tuesday night. These are the guys."

He finished his report, hung up the receiver, and turned to Marr. "If we had a few more men like you who would shoot at these stickups," he said, "and shoot to kill, we'd have fewer stickups."

Marr said gently, "I hated to shoot, but everything I have in the world is tied up in this station."

Vivian Starling moved up to stand close to Jerry Marr and said, "We found your car parked in the middle of the block at the Tollman house. When we couldn't raise anyone at the house, I figured something might have happened and they'd caught you. I told Frank we'd come here and made him promise that if we couldn't see any trace of you here he'd notify the police."

Jerry squeezed her arm. "Good girl," he said.

Gost was saying to the officer, "We saw the whole business. If you need any witnesses . . ."

"We won't," the officer assured him grimly.

The morning newspapers praised police for a solution of the Dixmer murder. Police, it seemed, had been on the trail of the murderers, a strange pair who lived a Dr. Jekyll and Mr. Hyde existence, operating a hardware store by day and engaging in nefarious criminal activities by night. Just before police caught up with them, they had tried to hold up a service station. The proprietor of the service station had held them off until police could arrive on the scene.

Jerry Marr tossed the newspaper on Gost's desk.

Gost said, "It was nice work, Marr. You showed excellent judgment in keeping me out of it. Suppose we say another thousand?"

"Five thousand," Marr said.

Gost looked at him in surprise. "Are you crazy?" he asked.

Marr's stare was steady and cold. "Listen, buddy," he said. "I've got a half nelson on this depression. Don't think I'm going to let up on it now."

"And don't think I'm Santa Claus," Gost flared. "I don't suppose it's ever occurred to you, but you've been just a little *too* smart. You could never connect me with that case now. Both men are dead. That holdup story was swell, but— Well, Marr, I'm the one who fixes the value of the services."

Marr said wearily, "I wish you wouldn't be like that. You'll make me lose confidence in my fellow men."

Gost said hotly, "It's business. You and I are dealing at arm's length. You came barging in here and wanted this job. I didn't hire you. You wished yourself on me."

"And a good thing I did," Marr said.

"We'll let that pass," Gost retorted. "The point is that there's nothing confidential in our relationship. We don't owe each other any good faith. We're dealing at arm's length."

Marr said dreamily, "I took a lot of risks."

"That's your business."

"I know," Marr said, "but while the cops were looking up the car registration and trying to find who those chaps were, and burning up the wires to San Francisco to find out about what had happened to the owner of the car, I had a chance to go back to that house."

Gost said, "Good heaven, what did you go back *there* for?"

Marr said, "I thought I might find a letter or two. That was a pretty strong letter you wrote her, Gost. You said, 'If you don't let up on me, I'll kill you.' Remember that?"

Gost sat bolt upright in the chair. "Hell!" he said. "I'd forgotten about that letter."

Marr took a letter from his pocket. Gost reached across the table to grab for it. Marr pushed him away. He held the letter in his right hand out away from the desk.

"You're the one that called the turn, buddy," he said

softly. "We're dealing at arm's length. If you want that letter any closer, you know how to get it there."

Gost sighed and reached for his checkbook. "You're costing me five thousand dollars," he said, "but I don't suppose I'd have had any respect for you if you hadn't."

Marr, still holding the letter at arm's length, grinned and said, "And I wouldn't have had any respect for me if I hadn't."

Gost carefully blotted the check, tore it out, and held it out at arm's length from the desk.

Marr grinned. Slowly the two men swung in their chairs until their extended arms met, Gost taking the letter, Marr taking the check.

The two men shook hands. Gost said, "I'm going to have some more work for you. Miss Starling has a friend she's going to send in."

Jerry pushed back his chair, shoved his hands down deep into his pockets, walked over to the window, and stood looking out. Abruptly he turned to face the broker. "Okay," he said, "it's going to cost dough. I've got this depression licked right now. I'll give you service you won't get anywhere else, and I'll charge accordingly."

A faint smile twisted the corners of Gost's mouth. "I was afraid of that," he admitted.